LOVE CAME
UNEXPECTEDLY

RUTH SCOFIELD

**Steeple
Hill®**

Published by Steeple Hill Books™

STEEPLE HILL BOOKS

Steeple
Hill®

ISBN 0-373-87296-8

LOVE CAME UNEXPECTEDLY

Copyright © 2005 by Ruth Scofield Schmidt

www.SteepleHill.com

Printed in U.S.A.

If you wish to remain in Me and My words remain
in you, ask whatever you wish,
and it will be given you.

—John 15:7

I wish to thank Tom and LuDawn Rodman
for their ever-present enthusiasm for the
Lake of the Ozarks, the boat rides, jet ski rides,
parasailing and their love of family. Your help
is always there and valuable. Thank you.

Chapter One

Grant Prentiss, without becoming obvious, stood near
enough to watch the young woman as she talked with
that Realtor, Jim Lindberg. Grant hoped she'd view him
as just another idler, someone interested in the water and
docks. That is, if she paid him the least bit of attention.
He didn't want her to think he was overly curious.

Though he was.

He'd give a good yahoo to know what Jim Lindberg
wanted. Although that was obvious enough. Jim Lindberg was a Realtor and if he wasn't offering his services
to sell this place, Grant would eat his favorite ball cap.

He wore a straw cowboy hat now. Without thinking,
he removed it to brush back his dark hair. His hand
came away damp with sweat before he replaced his hat.

Was the Realtor telling her what the resort was truly
worth? Some sky-high figure, no doubt. Resorts like
Sunshine Acres didn't stay on the market long, but the
reality was usually lower than what was promised.

Besides, the resort was old and the cabins needed updating, though honest repairs were at a minimum.

Sunny Merrill had inherited this resort. Its location and large acreage made it a prime property in spite of its aging cabins. She hadn't wasted any time getting here after notification, he thought. She'd hardly had time to properly look at Sunshine Acres.

But she couldn't sell it. Not right away, at least.

Grant surreptitiously glanced their way again.

Sunny Merrill looked like a bright summer day, with golden hair falling straight down around her shoulders, and gorgeous long legs showing under dark tan shorts. She was well named, he thought. She was rather tall, and he wondered where she'd stand, measured against him. Skinny as she was, she had all the right curves.

The two moved closer, down the slope toward the water. He prayed they would stop at the shoreline and not come onto the docks. He knelt and pulled his boat motor from his boat. It needed a cleaning, something he'd do later after supper.

Glancing again, he saw they had paused. He sighed—he wasn't quite ready for introductions.

She probably wasn't as pretty up close.

He glanced from the side of his vision, which told him nothing. She had a small straight nose and large eyes. He couldn't tell what color.

She didn't look like old Nathan much. But kids didn't often look like their grandparents, did they?

Where had she been all this time? he wondered for the hundredth time. Yet he knew. They'd found her in

Minneapolis. She worked in private practice as a charge nurse, she was twenty-six years old and she lived alone.

That didn't really answer his question.

But true to predictions, she'd come flying down to the Ozarks as soon as she heard about her inheritance. Oh, she'd driven in today, not flown. But she'd come, all the same, in a hurry. And now, what irked him to the hilt was that she'd contacted a real estate person right from the get-go.

Yet she had to contact Mr. Windom, the lawyer, at some point, didn't she? To collect the keys and pick up whatever else there was to pick up?

They turned toward the docks, so Grant put the motor down and casually strolled to docks' end. He watched a jet ski come in, way too fast, sending waves rippling his way to rock the wooden dock. This was usually a rather quiet cove, more filled with fishermen, isolated on the land side by a gravel road through huge stone cliffs and uncharted timber.

They didn't get many jet skis or water skiers here. Their clientele was quieter. People—customers—often came in by boat; the old gravel road took longer.

He listened as one voice grew more distinct. The Realtor's. He tipped his head, listening.

"The docks are your best asset," Jim said. "They are in good shape and you have a lift that works. Someone has been seeing to these things. Now if you put a little money into the cabins, I can get you top dollar."

"I'll think about it," she said.

She spoke in a rich contralto, a soft voice that had enough charm to easily lull bees and bunnies. It buzzed along Grant's nerve ends like rich dark honey, and he realized it could lull him, too, if he wasn't careful.

"Willis can do anything you want done. He's reliable."

"I appreciate your coming all the way out here with me, to see the place, Mr. Lindberg." She spoke smoothly, as though she was used to dealing with high pressure. "But I'm just not ready to make up my mind. The lawyer told me I needed to live here a year to inherit and I haven't decided what I'm going to do yet. I have a job I have to decide about, too, you know, and I've hardly had time to assess anything yet. Or evaluate it."

Determinedly, Grant thought he might as well get it over with and meet the new owner. He had to do it sometime. Besides, it wouldn't hurt to let Lindberg know he was around.

He moved toward them. Casually, as though he had nothing more on his mind than meeting his new neighbor.

"Hi there, Grant," Jim turned at his approach and spoke in his bright voice, apparently not at all surprised to see him. "Going fishing this evening?"

"Hi, Jim. Nah, just checking my motor. Needs cleaning. Too hot to go fishing anyway. Though I may take a dip."

"Grant, I'd like you to meet old Nathan's, um, granddaughter, the new owner of Sunshine Acres. Sunny Merrill."

Grant let his gaze swing her way; he wanted to look directly at her. He wanted to see her face at closer range. He wanted to see if she was really as pretty as she seemed.

Her cheeks were high and pale with little makeup, with a wide, barely lipsticked mouth. Her eyes were hazel, as he recalled her grandmother's being, a soft green-brown color.

His gaze settled on her mouth. She had the wide shape of Nathan's mouth. Startled at the knowledge, he barely registered the tired lines around her eyes.

He remained silent. Then realizing she expected him to say something, he spoke.

"Hi. Grant Prentiss." He held out his hand and she reached to meet it. Her fingers were firm beneath the soft skin. "I own Grant's Retreat."

At her blank stare, he added, thumbing over his shoulder, "I'm your next-door neighbor. It's a riding stable. I've only been up and running this last year, and your granddad helped me get underway. In fact, he sold me the land. I, uh…I really appreciated his help along the way."

"That's nice." She said it automatically. Without meaning.

Well, of course. She'd have no attachment to old Nathan. Not like he did. It meant nothing that Nathan—

He shut down his thoughts. That way led to disaster. He'd better leave it alone.

"Well, I guess you'll let me know," Jim said reluctantly, as though if he let her go without a firm commitment, he would lose a sale. "In any case, I want to welcome you to the Ozarks and the lake. After you get settled in, maybe we could have lunch one day next week."

"Perhaps."

"Okay, then. Just come by or call. I'm usually

around." Jim walked down the dock and then disappeared up the stairs and over the horizon.

Grant was glad to see him go.

Quiet reigned. Grant tried not to stare at her, but he was losing the battle.

He drew a deep breath. "I guess you'll want to look around. I know this place as well as I know my own. Grew up coming here, summers. I can point out…"

Her eyes were glazing over. "Um, want me to guide you?"

There was a tightening to her lips.

"Mmm… I don't think I need you, thank you. I'll just find my own way about. Mr. Lindberg says the owner's cabin is the gray one?"

"That's right."

"I'll have a look at that. And maybe find a bed."

They walked off the docks and up the concrete stairs. The noise of the jet ski had faded, and the place was filled with only the sighing of the wind and the chattering of the birds. Silent without guests. Peaceful.

"Have you ever been down to the Lake of the Ozarks before?" Grant asked.

"No. I've heard about it, of course. Some of my patients have talked about vacationing somewhere on the lake. I seldom paid attention because I've always been so busy. Never thought I'd be in the position of owning a resort, though. It's quite large, isn't it?"

"The resort or the lake?"

"Um, both, I guess."

"Oh, yeah," he answered slowly. "Okay. Um, the Acres consists of about forty acres, with a lease on more

of the timber." He swung an arm up, pointing to the tim-
bered hills. "There's about forty-eight acres of timber,
too rough to do a lot with, edging my land."

"That's very nice." She said it as though he were
talking of the moon.

"Not too many isolated places like this one left. This
is one of the reasons this property is so valuable."

"So I've been told. Look, it's very nice of you to tell
me all that, but—"

"No buts to it. That's why I wanted to talk with you
as soon as possible. You see, I had a deal with your
granddad. If you're going to sell Sunshine Acres…that
is, after your year is up…well, before he knew about
you, he promised to sell the place to me."

She stopped outside the gray cabin. She studied him,
stared into his eyes a long time.

"You know a lot about my situation, don't you?"

"Enough." He nodded, wondering what she was
thinking, *how* she thought, the processes of her brain.
"I know you are an unknown quantity—a newly discovered granddaughter. A nurse from Minneapolis. Old
Nathan was a friend of mine."

"A close friend, hmm?"

"I guess you could say that."

"Yes, I…understand. Well, Mr. Prentiss," she said
coolly. "I can't make any decisions for a year about
selling, but when I do, then I'll entertain all offers. By
a year from now, I'll have this whole thing under control. Now if you'll excuse me?"

She unlocked the door, went through, and closed

it in his face. Grant stood a moment, startled at her rudeness, then angrily wheeled away. What a cold package!

From the other side of the door, Sunny heard him leave. Sighing, she closed her eyes a moment. All this was strange, totally new, and nothing had prepared her for it. It was nothing like her life back home, with work, and study, church and visits with the Larsons.

Nothing like knowing she was alone. This inheritance gave her a strange identity, a different understanding of herself. She felt she had to learn a whole new side to who she was and where she came from.

Finally, she turned to view the cabin she'd be living in for a year. Alone.

Alone and…managing. Everything was quiet, the quiet of deep hush. She listened for traffic, for a radio or television from another apartment, for far away, unseen voices, but all she heard was the breeze.

She glanced around. Was there anything left of her grandfather here?

Sunny laid the keys on the deep blue-speckled counter beside the door. The cabin was divided into two sections; the front was an office, and she presumed the back was the manager's living quarters.

She turned to look at the office. A huge desk, knee-deep in clutter, sat next to a large window; she'd have to go through that the first chance she had. No telling what was there. Opposite the desk sat two comfortable office chairs against the wall.

To her left was the counter, which held the computer and phone. Both were about ten years old; she switched on the computer, and it immediately booted up. She marveled that it still worked. She shut it off; tomorrow, when she'd rested, she'd look into things more thoroughly.

Behind the counter was a wall of shelves stacked with brochures and other literature, and a cork board loaded with pictures. Hung from the second shelf down, at eye level, was a row of keys. For the six cabins, she suspected.

Tomorrow would be time enough to inspect them. They were empty and locked, and had been since the death of her grandfather.

She pushed through the door in the middle of the office and found herself in the living quarters. This is where her grandfather had spent his off time.

There wasn't much to it. A mid-sized room that was a combination kitchen, living room and dining room. A large window let in the dying light. There were a sagging sofa, a couple of dark-shaded lamps, an aged TV and a brand-new kitchen dining set of medium oak.

Along the wall sat shelves of books—years and years of publications, mostly popular fiction.

She strolled over to run her eyes over some titles. Many were from early in the 20th century. Nathan liked Westerns. It figured.

From the living room, a back door led to a modern deck. It had been added in recent years, she concluded, and was set with a variety of chairs. She decided this was where her grandfather had entertained.

Adjacent to the living room were the bathroom and a tiny bedroom, just big enough for a bed, a small chest of drawers and an equally tiny closet.

She found a well-placed wall lamp above the bed, and clean sheets on the bed. How odd…that old Nathan would leave the bed ready for a different occupant.

Or that someone had.

An open book, a Western, lay face down on the bedside table.

A few old clothes still occupied the closet. Were they her grandfather's clothes? They must be. Had he worn this old shirt? She touched it, a faded brown plaid, and took it from its hook. It was clean but wrinkled.

She held it to her nose. It smelled of laundry soap and the breeze that had dried it.

Unexpected tears welled up, and she buried her face in the rumpled shirt. Where had they come from? She held the shirt away again. The tears rolled down her cheeks.

She had never known her grandfather.

"Oh, mercy. This won't do." She hadn't expected them at all, and she swiped at them with the back of her hand. How she wished she'd had a chance to meet her grandfather. If she'd known…

But she hadn't. She'd been told about her father, Johnny Merrill, and how Alison, her mom, had loved him. She had heard all about their runaway romance, and how Johnny'd died in an accident before Sunny was born. Her gentle mother had been heartbroken.

Her mom had spoken of him with lingering affection and love in the days of Sunny's growing up, but they'd lived from hand to mouth. Alison never told Sunny anything about Johnny's parents.

What her mom had said was that there were no living relatives. Sunny had assumed they were all gone, like Mom, now, to cancer, and her mother's parents, to a heart attack and an accident. Like her dad.

She sighed. Alison had died when Sunny was twelve. Sunny had finished her growing up in foster families, some better than others. But she'd been blessed beyond reason when she'd finally fallen in with the Larsons at almost fifteen.

They'd helped her grow to womanhood and Sunny visited them now every week, along with their current crop of foster kids. She especially loved little Lori.

Well, this was her inheritance. She sniffed back her tears and straightened. After the inspection, she had intended to go back to town to a motel and to have a good dinner. She'd driven since early morning, from Minneapolis, and she was exhausted.

But that was changed now. She'd sleep here. She put the shirt back in the closet.

Sunny set about unloading her car. It was almost dark, and she turned on all the lights in the cabin as she traipsed back and forth carrying her things inside. There wasn't much; she had packed for only a couple of weeks. She'd planned to stay only until she could understand where she stood with all this.

But the lawyer said she had to live here a year…

She wouldn't think of that now. There were immediate things that demanded attention. The stack of bills she'd spied on the desk and counter, for one.

Bills made her comfortable. After all, she'd been paying them since she'd turned sixteen, and at twenty-six she felt comfortable and disciplined taking care of them. She'd worked steadily, first as a nurses' aide, then at anything she could find while she went to school. She'd been in fast food, first a fry girl, then a waitress, moving from one restaurant up to another where the tips were better. She'd saved every penny she could to go to school. She still owed on college loans, but she was paying them off a little at a time.

First thing tomorrow, after she'd made an inventory of the entire place, she would know where she was with it all. She'd never lived outside a city before, and the idea began to make inroads on her mind.

Only squirrels could be heard…and the lapping of the lake. Crickets began their song. The dark outside was vast and enclosed everything.

She hurriedly locked her car, then went inside the cabin and locked the outside door. There, that was better. She checked all the windows, finding two unlocked.

"Imagine, leaving the place so vulnerable," she mumbled aloud, thinking of thieves and rapists and murderers. She turned each lock with precise care.

There were no shades on the office windows; anyone out there could see into the cabin. Biting her lip, she closed the door connecting the office and living quarters. Tight and cozy at last, she finally sank into a kitchen chair.

It was quiet.

Jumping up, she switched on the television. There was a big satellite dish by the side of the cabin. Reception…

…was minimal.

She flipped from channel to channel, but there wasn't enough to catch her attention. She sighed her disappointment and turned it off. She might as well see what was in the cupboard. A can of soup would do for dinner.

She found several. Tomato, beef barley, vegetable. She had a choice.

The refrigerator switched on, sounding loud in the silence. She nearly jumped out of her skin.

"Oh, I'm being silly," she said aloud. "This is mine now. I'll get used to it, won't I, Granddad? I can even learn to fish if I want to, and go boating. And when I sell the place, I'll pay off my school loans and help the Larsons…"

She laughed at herself. If her granddad were alive, would he think her crazy for talking to herself?

Most people would. It would be better to think of that Grant guy to get herself in the proper frame of mind. She imagined herself recounting her adventures to the Larsons. Grant was good-looking enough to appeal to most females—and he wore a cowboy hat.

Yeah, he sure was good-looking. And he had great eyes, though they stared at her with suspicion. Never mind. She just wasn't interested in dark-headed cowboys right now. She had more important concerns about her future, not romance.

Chapter Two

She woke suddenly. For half a moment, she was confused about where she was. A whispering drifted from her half sleep, seeping away as she woke. What had she heard?

She lay silently, listening for something…

A motor boat, far away, made her aware of where she was—a place completely different from her apartment or the busy hospital or doctor's office she knew.

Faint light sifted around the edges of the curtains. It was morning? Time to get up and going on the day. She had so much to do she hardly knew where to start.

Jumping from the bed, she padded to open the door to the office. Her quick inspection of the kitchen the night before hadn't unearthed a coffeepot, so she'd have to make do with the one she'd spied on the metal file cabinet in the office. She suspected it was kept there to supply guests when they stopped by.

The office was full of light, though the sun was just

beginning to send rays through the front windows. She blinked into the sunlight. It was later than she'd thought.

The coffeepot sat on a hot plate. She hurriedly tip-toed over to grab it before she realized she was alone. There was no need to remain quiet.

Someone rapped on the front door. In the quiet, it sounded more like pounding.

"Eeek…" She squealed and jumped a foot, her heart beating hard. Who was at her door? Already? She wasn't ready for company. She was in her shorty pj's.

Which reminded her there were no curtains on the office windows. Anyone could look in and see her. The fact that she was no longer in a city with busy streets and crowded hallways did nothing to calm her. That was what she was used to.

She scurried back through the inner door, closing it behind her. Whoever was at the outer door could just wait. Or go away, she didn't care. Imagine expecting her to be on call at the crack of dawn!

The knocking continued.

Grabbing her lavender summer robe, she slipped it on, then hurried barefoot to open the office door.

The tall guy from last night stood there…what was his name? His gaze went from her tousled head to her painted toenails, noting where the robe stopped at her knees. Why did he make her feel she was exposing more than she should? Her robe covered more than a pair of shorts did.

"What is it?" She asked rather grumpily. Her temper made her impatient and cranky. Then her training kicked in. She cleared her throat and said more evenly, "May I help you?"

He raised a brow, an amused grin starting to spread.

"I thought since this is your first morning here, you might like to go out to breakfast."

"Well, I don't know…um…?" She stumbled for his name. She usually remembered people's names, but at the moment his mischievous look distracted her.

"Grant." His smile spread wider.

"Ah, yes. Like the Civil War general."

"As a matter of fact, that's the way it was. My grand-dad is a history buff, and he named me."

"Oh, is that a fact?" She was interested in spite of his silly grin. No one knew much about *her* personal history.

"How about breakfast?"

"I suppose it couldn't hurt." She was starving. There wasn't anything in the refrigerator except mustard and ketchup, and the soup from dinner the night before was long gone. She'd have to grocery shop at some time, she knew. "Give me fifteen minutes to get ready."

She turned, and raced into the bedroom.

"Fifteen minutes?" He called after her. "Most women take that long just to get into the shower."

She heard him, but she didn't answer. She'd been trained to take three-minute showers, and two-minute dry-offs. Getting dressed was a matter of grabbing the clothes off the top of the stack in her suitcase.

True to her word, she reappeared in the office in fifteen minutes. She wore jeans, a blue T-shirt, and brown sandals. She'd combed through her wet hair with the speed of lightning, and twisted it up with a large clip. She wore no makeup.

"I don't believe it," he said, looking at his watch, then

giving her a once-over glance. "Fifteen minutes to the second."

"I never usually take long," she said with a note of pride. "But for breakfast, I put a rush on it. Where are we going?"

It didn't matter a whit. She could eat a cow. Maybe two.

"There's a place about ten miles that way that's good."

She had no idea where "that way" was. She supposed he was safe enough. He escorted her out to the road where a small red pickup was parked.

"Now tell me, where did you get the name Sunny?"

"My mom named me Sunny because she said the day I was born was the sunniest day she'd ever seen," she said, climbing into the truck. She did know that much, at least.

"What did your dad say to that?" He closed her door, then went around to his side.

Sunny shrugged. "I don't know. He died before I was born."

"That explains it."

"Explains what?"

"Oh, um…that your granddad never said…never knew about you. I guess the communication got lost along the way somewhere."

"Yes, I suppose so." She didn't want to discuss it, not with this near stranger. Her emotions were too on edge. "Tell me about the lake and its history."

"Ah…that's a tall order." And a safe one. "All right, here goes. In the thirties, the local utility company built the lake to generate electricity, and since it's a private concern, that's why anyone can build right on the lake…"

Grant talked all the way to breakfast. She watched him shift gears at a crossroad, barely glancing to the right and left. Then he talked through breakfast, and she watched his expressive eyes as he told her of the struggles of the utility company to obtain all the land.

At the end of their meal, he slowly wound down. He'd eaten his eggs and sausage, while she nibbled on the last of her toast, having consumed her meal without a word.

"Fascinating," Sunny said. It was a word she used when she didn't know what else to say in a given conversation. But she really meant it. The history of the region *was* fascinating.

"Well, now that you've got your tummy full, what are you going to do?"

"Go shopping."

His mouth drooped. "It figures. I never knew a woman who didn't want to shop all the stores in an area new to her."

"I meant for groceries. Where are the nearest grocery stores?"

His face brightened. "Really? Well, your best bet is about two-plus miles at the end of this road. You know, I could do with a bit of grocery shopping myself. Why don't I take you now? It would be silly to go all the way back to Sunshine Acres only to pick up your car."

She studied his face. Did he really have nothing better to do?

"What about your resort? Don't you have riders...er, customers arriving?"

He glanced at his watch. "Not likely today. But it's

early yet. If we shop quickly, I won't be that late getting back. Besides, I have someone there to take care of anyone that might happen by."

"Oh, that's nice. You have an assistant."

"Yep. His name is Buzz."

"All right, I suppose. I appreciate the help."

The grocery store was a small one, but she chose several frozen entrées and lots of fresh vegetables and fruits. Grant settled for coffee and steaks.

On the drive home, Grant talked of his plans for Grant's Retreat.

"I hope to expand to three trails a day in the summer. It would be great, if I can continue to trail the extended ride through the forest. And in autumn, I plan to host some evening rides. But I just got going before the end of last year…nobody but my family came for rides, practically. Old Nathan has been…was wonderful about waiting for payment while I'm getting started."

"What do you mean? About my grandfather?"

"He owned the land. Didn't you know?"

"No." She watched the ribbon of road twist and turn while he talked.

"Yeah. And then there was a ten-acre partial in the valley that attaches to mine that he had an eye on. It made a solid bridge to mine. He called me as soon as it went on the market. I was able to snap it up."

"I see." Childish, unreasoning jealousy welled up inside her. Jealousy and envy over knowing and spending time with Nathan, really knowing her grandfather. How did this stranger rate so fine a treatment from someone who… Nathan was *her* grandfather? To spend days with him, to hear him talk, to know how he moved, how he went about his work, to know what he liked to eat?

Grant glanced at her, his lashes flickering her way. He spoke more softly. "I guess you do. Nathan…was a fine man. None better."

They'd reached her place, Grant parking along the road. Sunny wrenched opened the door as soon as he halted the truck.

"Thanks for the breakfast and the grocery run," she said formally. "I must go now. There's a lot of papers to read and…other work to do."

He unloaded her bags and set them by the door, glancing curiously at her face. "All right. I gotta go, too. I'll be seeing you," he said in parting.

But Sunny was already searching for her key.

She tried to shake off the feeling as she pushed through her door. It was ridiculous, feeling jealousy. That she hadn't known her grandfather was no one's fault—only a fact of life. It couldn't be helped. She shouldn't feel jealous…but she did.

She heard the disappearing motor, not paying much attention to Grant's leaving.

After years of neglect, how could she not feel such…hurt? Her grandfather had been alive during all those years she had struggled, when she had needed family. And she hadn't known of him.

Pain shafted all the way down to her toes.

Irrational anger raged suddenly, something she'd never experienced before in her life. How could her grandfather have been so close to Grant? Close to a stranger? As though those two were the ones related, and not her. Leaving her out.

Lord, I need Your calming spirit... I don't know why I feel such rage...and hurt, too. I shouldn't. It's so self-ish and irrational... I'm an adult now and should be be-yond such feelings. Nathan couldn't have known I even existed before a few months ago, and that's no fault of his. I guess it's Mom's fault, if anyone's.

With all of her might, she shoved the feelings down. In her mind, she quietly quoted Scripture to accomplish the task, something she'd done since her childhood.

"The Lord is my strength and my shield; my heart trusts in Him, and I am helped..." came to her from Psalms.

Never mind. She had work to do.

The phone was ringing, and she didn't think she'd connected the answering machine before she'd left. She hurriedly set the groceries down, then grabbed the phone.

Someone was calling about rates.

"I'm so sorry, I've just begun working here and I can quote you only what this card says...." She listened a moment. "No, Sunshine Acres will be closed until the first of the month due to..." she couldn't say the words, due to the fact that her grandfather had died.

"A...family problem." She listened again, hearing a desire to know when Sunshine Acres would be open again, asking someone to call. "I'll do that."

Sunny put away the groceries, and then sat at the of-fice desk. She sorted and sifted through the weeks of mail, not knowing exactly what to do with the majority of it. Some she simply put aside to deal with later; confirmations and requests for reservations, she put into a separate stack.

She answered phone calls twice more—people who had heard of the resort's change in ownership, wanting to know if Sunshine Acres would continue, whether their bookings were still all right. She assured them that if they had made reservations, they would have the cabins in the time they'd requested.

Not knowing where the reservations book was located, she glanced about. Then she went to the computer. It booted up without a problem. She looked at the programs, then went to the e-mail.

Which was a mistake. There were tons of messages.

For the next two hours, she sorted through them, eliminating most, keeping some. Finally, she rose and stretched. She had to get out of the cabin…

Time to visit the guest cabins and see what shape they were in, she thought.

Taking the keys off the hooks, she glanced at them. They were old keys and she hoped they worked.

She pulled her door closed and locked it. Then she strolled down the concrete boat launch to the level of the cabins. There should be a separate path to each cabin from the car park, she thought. But the car park was nothing but a dirt patch of ground, sitting adjacent to the road. There were a few concrete steps to the manager's cabin, then, on the lower level were the six guest cabins.

All the cabins were alike except for color. None but one of them had basements; the rest were all on stone foundations. She stood in front of the first one, and took a deep breath. She placed the proper key in the front door and swung it wide.

One large room met her gaze; it was much like hers. It contained a strip of kitchen cabinets, old and dated, and a newer stove and refrigerator in white on the wall facing the road. The dining and living room were combined, with a large dining table and chairs taking pride of place in the center of the room. An iron daybed sat in the corner. A huge picture window looked out over the lake, giving a view that took her breath away. A bathroom and two small bedrooms filled with inexpensive furniture completed the cabin.

This was like a cabin of fifty years ago, she thought. Where were the furnace and hot-water tank?

She found those in the closet beside the door.

It seemed clean enough. Nothing had been touched since her grandfather's passing. But where were the laundry facilities? Was everything sent out?

Each cabin was alike, she discovered, as she wandered from one to the other, the only difference being the furniture that occupied them. The last cabin, built on a higher slope of land, had a lower level, which proved to be a boat storage. It was empty, but she thought it looked as if it had been recently occupied.

Sighing, she closed and locked the last door. There was only one building left to inspect. The huge garage at edge of the road, past which the drive wandered to her cabin, the office.

She stood and gazed at the garage. She decided it could wait for another day because she was exhausted. Everything—her quick response when she'd heard from the lawyer, to making arrangements to take a leave of absence from work, to coming here—everything was catching up to her.

Slowly, she strolled back toward the office. There was enough paperwork to keep her busy for the next two days. What should she do with it all? A number of people held reservations on cabins for stated times and weeks of the summer. Either she had to keep those, or refund the money.

And she hadn't yet found the ledger, nor any money, and the computer hadn't revealed a thing. So far she hadn't found a bank book, either. Oh, hang it. She didn't even know the banks in this area—something else she'd have to investigate. Surely Nathan kept operating money somewhere.

It was a much bigger problem than she'd imagined.
Oh, Lord, I need help…

Chapter Three

She had to keep the resort open. She had no choice.

Coming to that conclusion sometime through the night, Sunny woke with a set determination. It was only early June; there was the whole summer before her and customers to contend with. Some who had already missed their dates to come wanted their money back, and she had no idea where Nathan kept his accounts.

Perhaps those customers would accept a later date, with added days free, she thought. It was worth a try.

She had to start with this weekend, no matter what. The first thing she had to do was call her supervisor. Would her boss hold her job for a whole year? It wasn't likely.

She sighed in frustration. What did she know about running a resort? This was her first visit to the lake, for crying out loud!

Yet there were a dozen reservations...

Going through what papers were on the desk and

counter, she counted at *least* a dozen reservations for throughout the summer months. And she'd fielded one phone request yesterday afternoon. The woman was quite disappointed when she found she wasn't dealing with Nathan Merrill and that she couldn't be accommodated.

Just yet. Sunny would call her back this morning, she had written down her number.

Sunny rotated her shoulders and stood up to do a few exercises. She bent, knees locked, to touch the floor. Then she swung from side to side, her arms extended.

How hard could it be to take care of six cabins? During her teen years, she'd worked as a nurses' aide. She'd handled every job thrown at her—including emptying bedpans, changing sheets, mopping floors and making people comfortable. She could do the same here.

Throwing on her clothes, she brushed her hair and then braided it in one long braid. She hadn't had time to get it cut before she left Minneapolis.

Thinking about the overall problems the resort had— *challenges,* her mom would've called them—she recalled her inspection yesterday.

All the cabins were clean and neat. Who had cleaned them and when? She hadn't found evidence of anyone who worked for Nathan. No paperwork on payment of cleaning services. Or lawn services, for that matter. The uneven grounds had been neat and trimmed, too.

Well, obviously, someone was employed to do the work. But where would she find their employment records? And the money to pay now?

Until she found out who, and if that service could be

continued, she'd have to manage by herself. And where were the lawn mower and other garden tools?

Grant would know.

Grant seemed to know a lot about her grandfather's resort. She hated to depend on anyone…but he'd said she could ask him whatever she wanted.

Grant hadn't been around since yesterday morning. Glancing at her watch, she saw that it was seven-thirty. Seven-thirty at a resort wasn't as early as in a busy nurse's schedule, but maybe at the lake…

She let her hand lie on the old-fashioned phone, and pressed her lips together. Did she dare call him?

Punching in the numbers quickly, she waited while the phone rang. He answered on the fifth ring.

Or rather, someone did. A gravelly male voice answered. "Grant's Retreat."

"Oh, um, is Grant there?"

"You bet."

"Well, may I speak with him?"

"Yep"

She heard a slight scuffling, then a breathless Grant came on. "Hello?"

"Grant?"

"Uh-huh…"

"Hi." She let her breath of relief out silently. "This is Sunny Merrill."

A pause, then he said, "Oh, hello. How are you?"

"Fine, just fine." She hoped she didn't sound too lame. Then remembering the slight muffled noise, she said, "Did I take you away from something?"

"Ah, no. Nothing important." It sounded as though

he was doing something as he replied, "What can I do for you?"

"Sorry to bother you, but, um, I was wondering…um, if you have time today, would you mind stopping by for a little while?" She wouldn't blame him if he wanted nothing more to do with her. She'd handled his previous offer badly. "I need a few questions answered, and I'm finding I need—"

"Advice?"

"Answers."

"What time?"

"It's seven-thirty-five."

"No…I mean what time do you want me to stop by?"

"Oh." It was a good thing he couldn't see the flush that stained her cheeks. Used to accounting for every minute of her day, she'd reacted with her usual quickness. "Sorry." She took a deep breath. "Anytime. I mean, I'm here all day."

"All right. I have a ride this morning to take care of. Almost time for it now, so they'll be here any minute. But I'll be through in a couple of hours. Could be at your place close to noon."

"Thanks, Grant. Noon. I'll…um, treat you to lunch. I appreciate it."

By noon, she'd sorted through the last of the mail. She'd found stacks of stuff, some of it from years past, but nothing of importance. Nothing to tell her who she could get to look after her docks and grounds. She'd checked the computer, but found little that told her what she should be looking for. Hadn't her granddad used it?

She'd found a few messages for Nathan, personal

messages that she hadn't the heart to read just yet. She didn't erase them, but put them in a separate folder for future reading. Maybe she'd learn something of her grandfather's personality from them. She supposed those people who had written had been given their own notification about her grandfather's passing.

Would they be shocked to know of her?

She heard a vehicle pull into the parking lot. The office door opened, and Grant swung through. Was it noon already?

For a moment, she stared at him.

She watched his lean body as he came in. He didn't look like a cowboy now. His tan shorts stopped above his knees and showed long, tanned, sturdy legs. His short-sleeved polo shirt, with a golf emblem on the pocket, displayed his muscular arms to perfection. His hair lay close to his head, dark with dampness. He looked as though he'd just stepped out of the shower.

After all the teasing she'd received back in Minneapolis from her nursing buddies about going to Missouri for a lake cowboy, she just wished she could point them to Grant now. Or take his picture to send back.

Cowboy indeed!

But he did look mighty fine, and she felt her heart ping in a dangerous way.

"Sorry I'm late," he said. "The guests lingered about, wanting to talk and look around. But I can give you all the time you need now. Don't have an afternoon ride today."

"It doesn't matter." She blinked, and rose. What kind

of guests? Single females? Females that appreciated his good looks?

What am I, nuts? Who has time for heart patters when I'm struggling to run this old place? It would only complicate things. Besides, I'm only going to be here a year. I can't get involved with him when I'm planning to go back to Minneapolis...

"I, um, thank you for coming," she said. "I've made sandwiches for lunch."

"That's fine." He stood with his thumbs hooked in his front pockets. "I'm starved. I didn't have much for breakfast this morning. Wanted to be ready for my riders."

"I didn't, either." She walked through to the living room, leaving open the office door for him to follow. She shoved her personal thoughts into the back of her mind—*I'm not into short-term romances*—and attempted to think of business. "Can I fix you an iced tea?"

"Yeah, sure."

"I have it made."

He took a kitchen chair as she busied herself on the short counter top. He was quiet, watching her fill matching glasses with ice cubes and tea.

Strangely, Grant felt a bit of alertness. Sunny Merrill didn't like asking for help, he'd noticed. She was uncomfortable with it.

"How's it been?" he asked by way of opening a subject she had a hard time approaching.

A difficult discussion, to be sure, but it was natural she'd want to know where everything was. Did that include bank accounts? What would she do if she found all of Nathan's accounts? Take the money and run?

She's not Heather, a little voice reminded him. *She's entitled to whatever Nathan left her. She could do as she pleased with it all.*

He pulled his thoughts back to what she was saying.

"Crazy. I had two calls yesterday to confirm reservations, and one requesting one." She handled the knife to cut the sandwiches with deft strokes, then put pickle chips on the side of the plates. "I handled them the best I could. But I've gone through all the papers and mail on the desk, on the counter, and stuff in the computer. I can't find how Nathan kept track of anything."

She glanced at him over her shoulder, her braid swinging. "How can you run a resort or keep track of it all, without a log or files or *something?*"

"Don't know. Nathan kept a lot of stuff in his head. He has—had—been doing this so long, he didn't have to write down everything."

"But that's loony. How did he do his taxes?"

"Don't know, but he had someone do them. I expect you'll find someone in town to answer tax questions."

She set a triple-decker sandwich in front of him. She put her own sandwich down, then stood by her chair, hesitating.

He glanced up into her eyes. Her gaze softly questioned him. "What?"

She let her tongue moisten the corner of her mouth. "I'd like to say grace before we eat."

Shock kept him silent for a moment. His family all went to church, and were faithful to their beliefs, but they'd never said grace at meals. He doubted they knew how.

He certainly didn't.

And he'd thought Sunny like Heather? Such a thing would have been very foreign to Heather's thinking. Yet saying grace was an easy enough thing to fake— maybe Sunny wouldn't really know how.

"Okay." He let his doubt rest.

Sunny sat down slowly, and bowed her head. Her hands were out of sight in her lap. She appeared tense, as though she didn't want to let another person—him— in on her personal thoughts. Or she didn't know what to say.

He watched the flutter of her lashes as she sought to form words. Then her voice softened.

"Father, we thank you for this food and the beauty of the day. Thank you for giving me…thank you…for all this bounty and for the many challenges, as well. Help me to meet them successfully. Please bless Mark Larson. Amen."

She raised her head, but didn't look at him as she lifted her glass of tea.

"This sandwich is delicious." He filled the silence with the first thing that came into his mind. She'd surprised him again. The bacon, lettuce and tomato sandwich was exactly as he liked it.

But who was Mark Larson? What did he mean to her? Was he someone waiting in the wings? A boyfriend?

"Thank you. I…hope I didn't…" she spoke quietly, gazing at her plate. Then her lashes swept up, and she looked directly into his eyes, her irises looking more green than brown. "I realize my faith can be awkward for some people. But in my own home, I can't ignore the need to ask His grace. And for now, this is my home."

He hadn't thought of that. In his mind, it still belonged to Nathan. He'd rattled around the old place for years each summer, and got to know old Nathan like another grandparent. "No problem. I've been known to ask the Lord for a favor or two a few times."

They munched for a bit.

"Now tell me what I can help you with," Grant finally said, figuring he would open the subject.

"Employees." She'd been waiting to ask. "I can't find a record of any, and I'm sure Nathan didn't handle everything by himself. Did he have someone to help him clean the cabins? And what about the laundry?"

"Hmm…he had several women over the years to do the cabins and the laundry after his wife died," he told her. "Sylvia and Anne something or other. Sylvia did them a few years till she quit to move in with her daughter. Then there was Anne."

"I haven't a record of an Anne. I found an old memo about Sylvia, I think."

"Well, Anne lives somewhere in town. Anne Newton. Somebody should know her." He took another bite of his sandwich, getting mustard on the edge of his mouth.

Her gaze settled on the spot, making him aware of his manners. His tongue edged out to swipe it, the taste sharp, and her gaze shifted elsewhere.

He guessed he'd passed muster at some point. She didn't seem as awkward with him now, or as uptight as she'd been yesterday.

"Okay. Where is the washer and dryer?"

"Oh, they're in the back of the garage. I'll show you after lunch."

"Okay." She was quiet again. Her hair looked golden in its tight braid, although tendrils of it had escaped and fluttered about her face. He had a sudden urge to brush it from her eyes, but kept his hands busy with his sandwich instead. He wondered what she did with her hair when she was nursing.

"Now, how about the lawns?"

"Nathan kept them up."

"Right." She nodded. "The place isn't big enough for full-time care, but I noticed they've been tended to recently."

"Ah, that was me." He stopped chewing for a moment, and swallowed. "I thought I'd just keep them trimmed until you turned up. I mean, nobody knew for sure if you'd even want the place, and I had the time. Nathan doesn't charge me to keep my boat here or anything—I mean, he didn't—"

"Yes, I see what you mean." Her gaze was speculative. "I have you to thank, then, huh? It's very kind of you."

"Wasn't much," he said in perfect cowboy lingo, then repeated, "I had the time. It's a fair trade. But soon my business will pick up and I won't have time for anything more."

Another pause. She appeared to be thinking that over.

"Okay. So now I'll have to find someone else to do the yard work." She put down her sandwich to take up her tea glass. "How about the boat stuff?"

"Boat stuff?"

"Yes, the, um…you know."

"Uh-huh. Well, Nathan took care of the docks, the boat lift, and everything else. He kept them pretty neat, too. I guess you can find everything you need—all the tools for keeping the place are in the garage."

"Active old guy, wasn't he?" she mumbled.

"Yep. Active as any ten men his age."

"Mmm…I haven't explored the garage yet." She raised an eyebrow. "Couldn't find the key to it. Do you know where it is and what's there?"

"Oh, the truck, I expect," he said, helping himself to sugar for his iced tea. He spoke without looking at her, and stirred his tea with vigor. "Ol' Winnie. And the lawn mower, wheelbarrow, hand tools. You know, the works."

"A truck?" Her voice went up a notch as excitement entered her system. She slapped what was left of her sandwich down on her plate, and looked at him with sparkling eyes. "There's a truck included? Really? What kind, what make?"

"Now hold on, it's not the Hope Diamond, you know. It's only a black truck. He always called her Ol' Winnie. She's about three years old, I guess."

"Yes, but I can turn in my rental car now. I won't have that cost and I won't have to depend on—I was using my savings—oh, never mind that now. A truck! And only three years old?"

It was the most excitement she'd shown.

"If I had known it would create such unbridled excitement, I'd have told you about the truck the other day," he said, letting his grin spread wide.

She glanced at him, flushed with embarrassment, and grinned back. Her mouth curved in such a way, it reminded him again of the way old Nathan's mouth made the same curve.

That was it. She had her granddaddy's smile.

Only on Sunny, it had a sweetness he hadn't counted on seeing. It charmed him out of his shoes. In spite of himself, or memories of Heather.

"I've never driven a truck, but I can learn. Ol' Winnie, huh? Well, how hard can it be? And it's only three years old. My old car barely got me to work and back, and I prayed every day that it would hold out just a little longer."

She finished her last bite, chewing thoughtfully, her eyes full of stars. Finally she turned to him. "Now what were we discussing? The yard?"

"Yeah, well, um, yard stuff… Nathan couldn't use a rider mower, you know. Ground isn't level enough. He walked the whole site, when his knee wasn't hurting him. The part that is kept mowed anyway."

"I guess I could manage that." She was a bit doubtful. Her voice grew pensive. "He had a bad knee?"

"Yeah. He, um, he'd get shots once in a while for it. He saw a doc in town."

"I see." Her face took on a still, faraway look again. Her mouth, in repose, was sweetly bowed. "Well, I suppose Sunshine Acres doesn't have much in the way of grass," she said, pushing back her chair. "But I noticed there were an awful lot of rocks."

"That's right, the soil is far too rocky for a real lawn, I guess." He chewed the last of his sandwich. "Gotta build up a layer of dirt if you want a lawn. Shirley had a few old flower beds when she was alive and could care for them."

Sunny turned to stare at him, a vulnerable, lost look

on her face that she couldn't quite hide. "You knew Shirley, too?"

"Yeah, a bit. Not as well as I knew Nathan."

"What…what was she like?"

"Oh, friendly…worked hard, but she liked to laugh. She had the kindest blue eyes I've ever seen. She loved being outside, and would stay out till dark most days. She loved talking with her customers. And she loved those flower beds."

Sunny was silent a moment, staring at her glass. Then almost as if she didn't want to ask, she did. "Did you ever meet my dad?"

"No."

The single word seemed to send her into stone. He was sorry he had nothing to tell her, but Johnny hadn't been in the picture when he'd come into Nathan and Shirley's life. Nathan hadn't talked of Johnny much. Shirley spoke of her son on occasion, but very little. His death seemed to cause her too much pain for long discussions.

Sunny shook herself, and smiled. "Will you have some ice cream?"

Chapter Four

The garage was huge, but the only vehicle in there was the shiny black truck, Ol' Winnie. Sunny stood and stared a moment. Her granddad really liked Ol' Winnie; the care he'd given the truck showed.

Was this really hers? Just a gift from the blue?

Not really from the blue, but it was another gift from a grandfather she had never known. Imagine…a truck!

"Wahoo!" She let out a shout. A truck would solve her most pressing problems.

Grant let out a chuckle. He observed her carefully, but she didn't care. Elated at finding a working vehicle, Sunny hoisted herself up and into the seat. She turned the key, starting the motor. It hummed like a top.

Her granddad must've enjoyed a good running engine, she mused. From habit she looked over her shoulder to make sure the drive was clear, then carefully backed Ol' Winnie out of the garage. Ol' Winnie, hmm… Secretly, she found her granddad's whimsy amusing. Naming the truck—it was an aspect of the old man she hadn't suspected.

She parked it, hitting the brakes a bit too hard, jerking her forward in her seat. Uh-oh. This truck would take some adjusting to.

"Wonderful! I'll have to get a pillow to put at my back," she crowed, looking at all the instruments on the panel in front of her. "And learn what all this means. Will you drive into town with me to return the rental car?"

She'd asked the question spontaneously, as though he had nothing better to do than help her. Glancing up at him from the seat, she held her breath.

"Sure," he said and nodded. The corners of his mouth twitched, and his eyes sparkled. It made her want to smile in return, but all she could do was stare at the corners of his mouth. "But we'd better do it this afternoon because I have things to do tonight."

"That's great timing," she caught her breath to say. "Then I can do some more grocery shopping."

She patted the steering wheel, then with resolve, got out of the truck. The rest of the garage was filled with tools, laundry equipment and the discarded treasures of a lifetime.

Turning her attention to the garage, she inspected the washer and dryer, whistling under her breath. "Boy, these are old. I suspect I'll have to replace them soon."

He watched her wander to the push lawn mower. "I suppose this is still okay…" She pushed it a few inches in its place. "And there are plenty of garden tools. I won't have to purchase anything new here."

Against the back wall was the work counter with cabinets beneath. Parts of boat engines, old life jackets, and a collection of various old license plates lined the wall. Didn't her grandfather ever throw them away?

She ran a hand down the counter. Her fingers felt the polished wood. A fine sand filled the corners. Her grandfather spent a lot of time out here, she thought.

She'd have a job to clean it up, but it would look tidy by another month, she vowed.

While she looked around, Grant lounged against the hood of the truck watching her. She tried not to notice, but she caught a quick, appreciative gleam when she turned to him.

Over the years, she'd dated a few men who'd openly admired her, yet she hadn't fallen in love with any of them. She hadn't had time, what with school, work and her church involvement.

Yet she didn't mistake Grant's gaze. She hardly knew what to do with it. Before now, her goal had been to grow up, study hard and make something of herself before getting involved with anyone. That drive had been constant.

The Larsons' influence had solidified her thoughts, too. Boyfriends could come and go if she wanted them, but the Larsons had encouraged her hard-working habits. They'd said that steady work, a solid career in something she was good at and her church would ground her.

And there would be no hopping from place to place, city to city for her, Sunny privately thought, not like the kind of life she'd led with her mother.

Her co-workers knew enough to keep their relationships just friendly. She'd keep this friendly, too, she decided.

She cleared her throat, then asked tentatively, "All right…can you go into town now?"

"I suppose so. Let me make a phone call, and I'll be set."

"Okay, you can use the phone in the office."

"I'll use my cell phone."

Of course. Most people had cell phones these days. Only Sunny, always saving money, did not. She really didn't need one, she thought, being so busy with work and with only a few friends from her work or church she could call on any available phone. Only her foster family mattered to her, and she called them most evenings from her apartment, assuring herself they were fine, that little Lori was fine.

That reminded her. She'd have to close her apartment. Could her foster father Mark do it for her? She owed him and Jessica so much already that she hated to ask him. Neither Mark nor Jessica were well these days, and they needed the money they got from caring for foster children. But she had no one else to ask and she couldn't leave the resort to take care of the matter herself.

She couldn't go on paying the expense of an empty apartment for a whole year, either. She'd have to trust someone to close it, like Mark and Jessica.

Grant used his phone while Sunny collected the paperwork on her rented car. It took all of five minutes.

"All set?" he asked from the doorway.

"You bet!"

Sunny drove the twenty minutes into town, with Grant following, and then the five minutes down the side street to the car rental at the side of the new-car lot. Grant turned off his motor and waited while she turned in the car. When she came out of the car-rental office, practically skipping, it made him chuckle.

"I never saw anyone so happy about a truck. Except your granddad, maybe, when he got it new."

"Well, a truck! I mean, I've never owned such a big vehicle before," she explained. "It'll take a lot of abuse, won't it? And I suspect it'll make it over these rougher roads just fine. A lot easier than that car did. And it will be big enough to haul washing if I have to take it into town. I'm not too sure about those machines."

He laughed. "I suspect old Nathan did that on more than one occasion. I'd see him sometimes, hauling his laundry around. Said he'd take it to town where he could drop it off at the Lite Laundromat, and he'd pay to have it done. Saved him some time and effort, I guess, especially if the housekeepers didn't show up. These last years he's been lonely without Shirley, and he…" he paused to run his tongue over his lips "…he sometimes liked the entertainment in town."

"Did he?" She grew quieter.

"Yeah…."

They were almost at the resort when he made a suggestion. "Sunny, I know you want to reopen the resort as soon as possible—"

"Yep, I have some people coming in tomorrow. It seemed foolish not to open it."

"Yeah, well, that's good. It's only good business sense. With reservations to honor and all, it shouldn't be too hard to fill it up."

He slowed his car, pulling into her drive, then stopped. "But why don't you give yourself some time about what to think…I mean, about your granddad? Whatever you do, don't make any quick judgments about your granddad, will you?"

He turned to look at her, his eyes serious. "He was a fine man. People liked him a lot."

Feeling warmed suddenly, she was grateful for Grant's friendship. She gazed at him, experiencing an emotion she couldn't name…but it was a welcome one.

"I…suppose they did. Thanks for that, Grant," she said softly. "And I wouldn't dream of making any quick judgments. Thanks for the ride into town, too. I owe you one."

His hand on the wheel, he spread it wide. "You don't owe me a thing, Sunny. But I'd welcome another invitation to lunch anytime."

"Sure." she said lightly, getting out of the car. "I'll let you know."

Grant drove on down the road. Sunny let herself into the small cabin, thinking about how sweet Grant had been. Sweet men made her a little suspicious—she didn't know what to think about Grant.

She refused to give her feelings about him any room to blossom. That would interfere with business.

She immediately turned on the air-conditioning unit. Old though it was, it was the only thing she had to cool off her room. She stood near it, raising her shirt slightly to get the cool air against her bare skin.

Heavenly…

The phone rang, and she dodged back into the office to answer it. It was a customer from Kansas City.

"Yes, that weekend is open for cabin number four. Hmm…what color is the cabin? Um, I think it's the, um, green one. In the middle. All right, from Friday night to Sunday. And the name?"

She was feeling quite comfortable with this. Her nurse's training had prepared her to deal with all kinds of people, and this was little different. She wondered what the nursing situation was down here, in this resort town. What was the small hospital like? Was it short of staff, as so many were?

By the time she'd taken a couple of more calls, and answered the ones from her answering machine, the sun was low. She left the cabin and wandered down the concrete path to the covered wooden dock.

She noted the remnants of her grandmother's flower beds that Grant had mentioned. She imagined them in full splendor. She'd sometimes helped Jessica plant flowers. She should do something about them. They would make the place much more colorful, make the place stand out a bit, make it more attractive.

Grant's boat lolled in the water, using one slip. It was a small runabout. She looked at it, noticing its wear, then moved on to inspect the other, now-empty boat slips.

She folded herself down on the dock's end, leaned back on her hands, and stared out. The day was losing its heat, and she lifted her face. A few boaters were out on the main body of water, which she could see. But her cove was quiet and serene. What would it be like with every cabin taken? And every boat slip filled?

The sun hovered above the water with its last blasting rays of the day. She watched it sink behind the hills, feeling peaceful. She sighed and strolled back to her cabin in the fading light.

She wouldn't admit to feeling lonely. Not even a tiny bit.

Going inside, she settled down in the office chair to make a very important long-distance phone call.

Dialing the Larsons, she leaned back and waited for an answer. They were as close to family as anyone she had. "Hi, Jessica, it's me, Sunny."

"Hi, honey. I'm so glad you've called. I've been a little worried about you." Her foster mother was a small woman with thin brown hair, but her heart was as big as all outdoors. "How's the heiress? Everything as good as you hoped?"

"Both better and worse...no, that isn't right. It's just different than I expected, that's all. And more work than I'd thought, but that's good. I mean, it's keeping me busy. But I've learned I really have to remain on the property and run the resort for a full year. There's no way to get around that."

"No kidding? So what are you going to do about your apartment? And your job?"

"I can't afford to keep them. I'll have to give them up. Can you and Mark go over and close the apartment for me? I'll write a letter to the manager, but I need someone to take care of what's there. Will you send me some of my clothes and put everything else into storage?"

"Sure, we'll do it, Sunny. You can count on us. You don't have all that much furniture anyway. Do you want me to ship you anything?"

"Only a few things. I'll send you a list. Tell me, how

is Lori?" Lori was the five-year-old mixed-race child she'd taken a shine to, the Larsons only current foster child. The child was adorable, with deep dimples and a smile that charmed everyone.

"Lori is just fine. She's asked about you several times. Wondered why you haven't been by lately."

Sunny chatted for twenty minutes, arranging the pack-up and storage of her things, then, mindful of the cost, she said goodbye and hung up. She sat a moment, praying for her foster family. Mark's job loss a few months back and his inability to find work again worried her. And Jessica's asthma made it hard for her to work full-time. How were they going to keep paying their bills?

Could they keep going until she sold the resort?

Her thoughts were unclear about selling. Surprisingly, she felt somewhat glad of the stipulation of spending a year here. She wanted to hold on for a while.

She rose, noting it was ten o'clock. She let her concerns go. Like Scarlett O'Hara, she'd have plenty of time to think of them tomorrow.

She enumerated what she'd have to do the next day. Calling her apartment manager in Minneapolis was first, to let him know the Larsons were coming to pack and ship her few things. Then check the cabins one last time before guests arrived. And so on...

She locked the cabin door and turned off her air conditioner, but she opened the bedroom window to let in air and kept her overhead fan going. The window air conditioner wasn't giving her much help. Getting into bed, she sorted through the books at her bedside. Choosing one, she started reading a Western.

She'd never before had time for fiction...

Long after she'd turned out the light, she awoke holding her breath, shooting straight up in bed. She had no idea what time it was. What was that sound? Footsteps? It couldn't be, the resort was empty...

Wasn't it?

Listening for a long moment, she heard nothing more than the whispering trees and faint lapping of water. She must be dreaming.

Breathing again, she began to relax.

But the sound of the lake lapping against the shore sounded louder than it should. As though something— a boat possibly—had disturbed the water.

The sound receded. Her eyelids drooped. She just wasn't used to the lake sounds yet, that was all, she reasoned. She'd become used to it...as of tomorrow, the resort would reopen and she expected three families and a couple of singles to occupy the cabins. There would be people here.

The next day, she was startled at how busy she was kept. Boy, were there people! Starting at ten, when the first family arrived, she heard the shouts and calls of children. She answered a dozen questions. She found herself busy in six different directions. When she saw two boats launched and occupying the slips, she unexpectedly felt relieved.

She was in business.

Then, when she had a quiet moment about seven that evening, she felt flat-out tired. But it was a good tired, a satisfying exhaustion.

Obviously, running a resort was no piece of cake.

On Sunday morning, she turned the television on to a TV preacher and listened to his sermon, but she found the preacher unsatisfying. Then her morning was interrupted by two phone calls, and someone wanting to find somewhere to eat Sunday dinner. She tried to accommodate them with brochures, then had to admit she hadn't a clue about what those restaurants really were like.

Sunday night when the first family left, she immediately cleaned the cabin. She changed sheets, scrubbed the bathroom and kitchen, vacuumed the place down. There would be new occupants on Monday, and she wanted everything to be clean.

She tried washing the sheets in the washer, but found the machine not up to the job. For the first time, she wondered what the health department would dictate. Were there any health-related regulations at all? She'd have to find out. Meantime, she'd have to take the sheets into town.

Another trip to town. What would she do with the customers when she went to town? What if someone wanted something while she was gone?

She'd have to take that chance.

By Tuesday, she wondered what Grant was doing. She'd seen his car drive past on Sunday evening. His employee was in the passenger seat, but all she saw of him was a gray head. He'd had his head turned. Where were they heading? She hadn't spoken with Grant since he'd taken her to turn in her rental car.

Thursday morning, she grabbed the phone as it rang on her way to clean another cabin. Thankfully, she heard Mark's and Jessica's voices.

"Hello, you two," her spirits lifted. "How are you? I'm so glad to hear a couple of familiar voices! I've been so busy, I can hardly even think."

"Are you busy? I wanted to tell you, we talked to your apartment manager today and closed the apartment. By the end of the month, you'll be free of it."

"Oh, thanks a million, Jessica. I owe you and Mark…"

She recalled saying that to Grant. Someone else she owed a favor.

Grant came into the office before she hung up. "Hi." She waggled her fingers at him, hiding her quickly beating heart. "Um, Jessica, I gotta go. Thanks a million for taking care of that matter. I'll talk to you soon."

She hung up. She missed Mark and Jessica and little Lori more than she could say. Perhaps they could come for a visit soon.

"Hi, Grant. What can I do for you?"

"Nothing important. I was just taking the boat out for a ride and wondered if you'd like to come along?"

She had yet to be out on the lake, and the idea excited her. "You bet! I'd love to go. But I'm worried about leaving the office empty before nine o'clock in case one of my customers needs something."

"You don't have to baby-sit them, Sunny." He said it as if that was a dumb idea—and, she had to admit, it was a little wacky. "If they need anything, you'll be back later. Put a sign in the window."

Still, she hesitated.

"You think that would be okay? I have to go into town tomorrow and I've been wondering how to do it.

You, know, run some errands, find a laundry and things. I—I haven't left this place since Thursday of last week."

It seemed like an eon ago.

"Sure, it's okay, Sunny. The customers don't expect you to be at their beck and call every minute of the day. You're not a prisoner, you have a life. Now let's go. The sunset is wasting."

"All right." That made sense. She grabbed a pair of sunglasses, a straw hat she'd found in the closet that she suspected had been her granddad's, and her keys. A tumble of things came down from the closet shelf, but she glanced briefly at it, then decided it could wait until she returned. She shoved it to the back of the closet.

A boat ride was just what she needed.

She'd never been on a boat before. She stepped in carefully, Grant's hand at her elbow.

Though there were people down at the boat dock, they merely waved to her. No one questioned her. After she donned the life jacket he pointed to, he started the engine and she relaxed against the back seat.

Grant steered the boat quietly out to the main channel, then pushed the speed higher. The wind whipped her hair behind her, cooling her warm cheeks and drying the perspiration against her neck. She placed a hand to hold her hat on, feeling the wind against her face.

What bliss!

Grant pointed out some of the more beautiful homes and buildings built into the hills and cliffs.

Staring at them, she noted that these homes ranged from luxurious to humble, and all the way between.

Sunny felt stunned. Before this, she had seen little of her community. Did people really live this kind of life?

"Grant, do you live here all year?"

He appeared strong at the helm, sitting with relaxed purpose, the late sunshine shining on his face. He turned from staring ahead of him. "I do now. I didn't before starting the stable. But I've been here two years."

"In the winter, too?"

"Sure. That's my quiet time. The lake is much more peaceful then."

"I imagine so, but…don't you get lonely?"

"Not a bit. There's things to do in winter. Catching-up things. Things you put off from summer. Even a few customers. You'll see."

Of course…yes…she hadn't thought of anything past getting the resort open, but she could imagine things she could do in winter. The stipulation said she'd have to live and work here a year. She understood that demand better now. What would it be like then, with no customers?

Well, like other things, she pushed those worries aside, trusting God to take care of them. Sighing, she decided she'd think about that tomorrow, too. At the moment all she wanted was to enjoy this wonderful, unexpected gift of a boat ride.

And the oh-so-pleasant company of Grant.

Chapter Five

Toward early morning, the clouds darkened and moved across the lake, shutting out any starlight. Lightning slashed low, disappearing into the lake, followed by a horrendous boom of thunder.

Sunny jerked straight up in bed, her heart pounding with the shock, just as another lightning flash lit the room for a split second. Then another, and a whooshing crash a short distance away.

What was that? A tree down?

In the black of blackest night, she knew there was no electricity.

Sliding from the bed, Sunny felt her way into the living room, and then toward the kitchen cabinets. She'd noticed a couple of oil lamps there. She fumbled around, knocking her shin, but finally found the lamps. Quickly, she lifted them down.

Now for matches. Were they in the drawer next to the fridge?

She felt a flashlight, and breathed a sigh of relief. She flicked the waning light on, decided it needed new batteries, and began groping in the drawer. There were some in the back, she thought.

Another lightning bolt helped her find the batteries. Deciding she could do with the lamps first, she found the matches. With shaking hands, she lit three matches, muttering "C'mon, c'mon…" before getting the wick to catch.

"Thank You, Lord," she muttered as the wick flamed high.

As quickly as she could, she replaced the batteries in the flashlight, and then hurried to the windows. Common sense told her to stand away from them with lightning out there, but curiosity as high as the sky sent her there to watch, just the same.

She could see nothing through the blackness.

Lightning illuminated the howling wind bending the trees low over the deck and rain lashing the wood. The chairs tumbled over.

I have to do something, Lord. I must.

She went into the bedroom and grabbed a pair of jeans. Setting the flashlight on the floor, she slipped into them, then grabbed a shirt from the closet. She dressed rapidly.

Please God, take care of my customers…and my docks. Don't let anything happen to the docks and boats. Don't let anything important be down.

A wave of fear washed over her. Were the folks in the cabins all right? Were they safe? She could see no lights. Dummy! Of course not. If *her* electricity was out, so was theirs. Was Grant's, she wondered? Were they on the same line?

What was happening down at the docks? Stepping tentatively out on the dark deck, she flicked on the flashlight, walking carefully down the steps. Her sneakers slipped on the rain-slicked stairs. The wind whipped her hair into a tangle and lashed her face, but she paid no mind. The dark blunted her light, making it difficult to see.

The place still held strange aspects, and she hated the need to check on everything. At home, tight in her little apartment, she'd have stayed under the covers. But Sunshine Acres was her responsibility whether she liked it or not.

She walked the short distance to the concrete stairs. Someone stood in the doorways at cabins three and four. She could see movement, something white against the dark.

There was no use in shouting. Whoever it was couldn't hear her over the wind. But it comforted her somehow, the presence of other people.

Thunder rolled down the lake, shuddering off the hills, bouncing down the water. The lightning was further off now, not so close.

The rain steadied with the dying wind. It smelled fresh, the way rain should. She hurried to the first cabin, which was unoccupied tonight, then to the second. "Are you folks all right?"

"Yeah, we're fine," answered the middle-aged man who had checked in two days ago. "That's quite a storm, though."

"Sure is. Okay…"

She hurried to the next cabin, finding that the folks had disappeared behind a closed door. All the other cabins were closed, as well.

The rain was lessening as the storm center rolled down the lake, but it didn't matter. She was soaked. She climbed the concrete stairs once more, shivering with cold, her fear receding, then turned to gaze at the docks below her just before she returned to her cabin.

Someone moved at the edge. Who was there? Something…or someone…

Her heart slammed into her chest in jerky beats, and she stood absolutely still, watching.

Movement down at the docks? Someone was watching *her!* She caught just a glimpse before the person was swallowed under the dock roof…

Who was there? Grant? Or a stranger? Surely Grant wouldn't be out in this storm….

She was out in it.

She didn't want to go down there, yet she was drawn down the stairs toward the docks. Standing on the edge of the last step, she listened.

She heard nothing beyond the storm.

But she *had* seen something. Was her imagination running away with her? She set her mouth and walked out onto the dock, all the way to the end. The rain couldn't get to her here. She inspected each of the four boats, one huge one, and the rest of various smaller sizes.

No one was there.

Each boat rose and fell with the rolling water, bumping gently in their moorings. They all looked serene.

She sighed and swiftly walked back to the path, then raced up the concrete stairs, and up her deck stairs to her back door. She was quickly through, safe and sound. She turned the lock decisively.

When she had stripped and dried off, her hair still damp, she put on another T-shirt she'd found in the chest. Then, exhausted, she climbed back into bed.

Only occasional rain patter could be heard now. Just as she was falling asleep, she heard the low hum of a motor. Whoever had been there, no longer was.

"There's a riding stable only a couple of miles down the road," Sunny said into the phone, thinking she had yet to see it. She wondered what it was like. She'd never been to one, and her curiosity climbed a notch.

Her curiosity had nothing to do with Grant, though. Nothing at all. It was all for what the stable was like.

Hah! An inner voice challenged.

She shifted her shoulders…and continued with *business*.

"I understand they can accommodate a party of ten to twelve experienced riders, at least. Inexperienced, they like a few less in their group, but—"

She listened to the male voice respond, then said "Mornings or afternoons?" Smiling because she'd sold them a package. Suddenly realizing she was taking on far more of Grant's responsibility than she should, she cleared her throat and said, "I tell you what. Why don't I give you the number and you can phone them yourself?"

Pleased, the caller said okay.

It was Saturday morning, and Sunny found she was

both irritated and pleased with herself by talking up Grant's stable with no trouble. She recited the number, already memorized. Then she reaffirmed the reservation at Sunshine Acres. "That's fine. We have you down for cabin five for next Friday."

That was the last cabin available for next weekend.

She hung up the phone and leaned back in her chair, tapping her fingers on the chair arm. Another Saturday. She'd been here over three weeks and the place was beginning to feel like home. She was tired enough at night to no longer mind the quiet.

But she had to have help or the place would fall to pieces around her. She didn't know how to clean the docks properly, the picnic tables under the tree should be moved, which took more muscle power than she could provide, and she wanted to put new screens on cabins three and four.

Oh, buttercups! As long as she was screening, she might as well have them all done. And the weeds were out of control.

Now for employees. At least one. If she went on at this pace, she'd be a basket case by the end of summer. She'd gone over her expenses. She could just about afford to pay one employee.

She looked up the employment place in the phone book, and before she could talk herself out of it, she punched in the number. Then she waited, holding her breath until someone answered.

"Lake Employment Agency. Molly speaking."

Sunny nervously stated what she wanted. She'd never hired anybody before.

"I have someone you can talk to this afternoon, if you want," Molly said. "Dell Jackson. He's been looking for work."

"Does he know life on the lake?" Sunny asked. "Would he be familiar with the work I want done?"

"Yes, I'd say so. Dell grew up here on the Lake of the Ozarks, and he's been around boats, water-skiing, jet skis, fishermen and such all his life. He knows it well."

"Okay, then. That's fine. You say I can interview him this afternoon?"

"Um, yes." Molly sounded a bit uncertain. "If I can get a hold of him."

"Well, I'm coming to town this morning," Sunny said in a staunch tone, "so I'll check with you about one o'clock. I need someone to help with the chores at Sunshine Acres right away."

Sunny ended the conversation with an upbeat feeling.

She'd go into to town, she decided, while all the customers seemed content with their own agenda. Do her grocery shopping and other errands, have a quick bite of lunch—she was tired to death of her own cooking and frozen entrées—and check out the employment place.

A church was in her thoughts, as well. She deeply missed services.

She'd take a quick drive around town to spot what churches the town held. Surely there would be a friendly church handy in town—she didn't much care what the preacher was like, she was only going to be around a year. She only wanted a place to worship her one and true Father. She'd try all the churches if need be.

Getting ready, she put on a bright blue sundress and brushed her hair till it gleamed. She might as well check out the medical facilities while in town, she reasoned. See what kind of nursing staffs they provided. Hospitals were always looking for nurses. Maybe she could get part-time work in the slower winter months.

Before she was out the door, the phone rang. Should she answer it or let the machine pick it up?

The temptation was too much, and she'd been trained to answer all calls. Sighing, she swung the receiver to her ear. "Sunshine Acres."

"That's twice now in three days," Grant said. She could hear the grin in his voice. "Thanks for sending those folks over my way. Many thanks. My business is picking up due to your enthusiastic advertising."

"Oh, did the folks make a date to ride?" she asked innocently. It was ridiculous how happy she was to hear Grant's voice. It gave her such a rush it made her nervous. "That's nice."

"Yep. For a party of five."

"I don't know how experienced they are."

"Mixed, the guy said. I'll take care of them."

"Good. Um, I hate to cut our conversation short, but I've got to run. I'm going into town this morning, and I don't want to be delayed. I'll see you."

"Hey, hey...don't be in such a rush." His voice took on a deeper tone. "I haven't talked to you in days."

"Yes," Sunny said, swallowing hard. "I know. But my window of opportunity to shop will be gone if I don't go now. I've got to arrange for laundry service or I'll go nuts doing it myself."

"Well, okay. But before you go, let me ask you…do you want to take in a show tonight?"

"A show?" She blinked. "Where?"

"Oh, there's an old-fashioned live performance about ten miles from here. They've been there for years. The people are all local talent. I like to support them, and some of them are actually pretty good."

"How…interesting. What kind of show?"

"Oh, musical, of course. It starts at eight. But then, we have a movie theater, too, where the kids hang out, if you want to catch a movie at the shopping center. How about it? Want to get out?"

"I guess so. Why not?" She said it hesitantly, but she desperately needed a night out and away from her responsibilities here. The invitation pleased her to no end. However, she was uncertain about closing the office and leaving her clients on their own and without anyone to come to if they needed something.

Not that anyone had yet. All her customers seemed to take care of themselves, once they checked into their cabins.

All at once, she made up her mind, and said more positively, "I'll go. When will you pick me up?"

"How about six-thirty?"

"Six-thirty it is. Bye now."

They hung up.

An employee was definitely on her list now. Someone who knew a little about lake society, and boats, and boat safety, and how to care for docks and…things. Someone she could put in charge when she was gone.

Pulling into the tiny lot at the employment agency in

due course, Sunny had to take a deep breath. She'd never interviewed a prospective employee before. But she tried to think of all the times she had been on the other side of the interview. Think about what this job needs, she reminded herself.

Swinging through the door, she saw the small office in detail. Behind a desk—old, but polished to a high gleam—sat a woman of about her own age. The woman's soft brown eyes glanced up as Sunny came into the room. "Hello. May I help you?"

"Hi. Are you Molly?"

"Sure am."

"I'm Sunny Merrill. I called earlier. I've come to see about someone to help at Sunshine Acres."

"Oh, yes, Miss Merrill. Dell should be along pretty soon. I phoned him right after you called me, and told him to be here at one, and it's just about that now. I hope that was all right. You said you wanted someone right away."

"Oh, I do. That was kind of you. You said his name is Dell?"

"Uh-huh. Dell Jackson." Molly sighed. "Poor Dell, he's just lost his father, and he's a little sad and lost for something to do. I shouldn't have told you that, but he's a neighbor, and I feel sorry for the kid."

"Oh, I'm glad you did." Sunny's heart softened. She knew about being orphaned from a young age. "Is his mother living?"

"No. Lost his mother years ago. He has a kid sister though, Tracy. They live with an aunt and uncle now."

"That's nice."

Sunny frowned slightly. There was a bit of caution

in Molly's voice. Was there more to Dell's story she should know?

"Anyway, Dell's a hard worker, he's lived here all his life, and he, uh, certainly knows boats and all. That's what you want, isn't it?"

"I surely do. I have to have someone reliable to take care of the lifts and docks and…and grounds and things."

As she was speaking, a young man of about twenty swung through the door. He stopped abruptly just inside, staring at her with deep blue eyes. His sandy bangs flowed almost into them, and when he blinked, strands of hair moved with his lashes. It gave him a rakish appearance.

Yet he looked clean and presentable.

He stuck his hands in his back pockets. He stood with an air of unspoken challenge that surrounded him like a thick lake fog.

"Well, here's Dell," Molly limply said from behind her desk.

"Hello." Sunny spoke tentatively. She didn't know whether to offer her hand or not, but since his were in his pockets, she thought not. "I'm Sunny Merrill."

"Hi."

"I own the resort, Sunshine Acres. I need someone to work part-time. To take care of the dock and lifts, and the grounds. Do you think you can do all that?"

"Yeah, sure. I've worked at Four Leaf Clover and Springers' in the past. And others for a bit while I was in high school. Took care of their boats, too. They can tell you."

"That's good." She let her breath out at the references

he offered. "You have lots of experience. I need someone right away. Do you…can you work tomorrow?"

He took his hands from his pockets and raked his fingers through his hair. It immediately fell back into his
eyes. "I can go this afternoon, if you want. Ain't…I'm
not doing anything."

"Do you know Sunshine Acres?"

Dell's eyes narrowed. "Yeah, I been there once or
twice. Even worked there for a few months. Old man
Merrill didn't like my radio tuned up loud. Didn't like
me to run his boat too fast. He was a grouch."

While watching Dell, Sunny carefully stored the information about her granddad. One more brush stroke
for the old man's personality. Dell seemed to resent her
grandfather's dictates.

She glanced at Molly. Molly bit her lip, quickly
glancing between the two of them.

Sunny returned her gaze to the younger man.

"How old are you?"

"Twenty."

She recognized a troubled soul when she saw him.
Dell was now twenty; even though he'd complained
about her granddad, he seemed calm enough now. She
wondered when he'd turned that corner. Six months
could make a huge difference in age, she knew, and
kids grew up. How long ago had he worked for her
granddad? Perhaps he had outgrown that rebellious
streak.

Or perhaps he hadn't. Hiding her sigh, she could
only hope so, anyway.

Molly intervened.

"Now, Dell, that was a while ago, wasn't it? Maybe you were too sensitive. And you're older now, so why don't you simply let all that go? Mr. Merrill liked his resort quiet and contained, and that's all right." Molly spoke soothingly. "Nothing to prevent you and Miss Merrill from getting along, now is there? Miss Merrill is offering honest work."

Sunny watched Dell's mobile face quickly fall into smoother planes.

So…he was willing to work with her.

"Yeah, I guess so. So do you want me or not?"

"Yes," she said, making up her mind. "If you're willing to work hard, Sunshine Acres needs you. You can start this afternoon? Can you come about three?"

Dell nodded.

"Okay, about three. I'll settle times and duties with you then. And if you're willing to work right away, I have a couple of jobs for you."

He nodded. "I'll be there."

Driving home after shopping and a drive-thru sandwich, Sunny thought about Dell again. She was relieved she'd found someone so quickly, yet she was also a little worried. He was a troubled kid if she ever saw one. She recognized all the signs from a dozen foster kids she'd grown up with and looked after.

If he proved difficult, she'd simply fire him, that was all. If he couldn't improve his attitude…

Yet she wasn't satisfied with that. Jessica Larson wouldn't be, and Sunny had learned a lot of life lessons from her foster mom.

Dell's attitude didn't have to predict his actual work performance, did it? She'd just have to wait and see.

She was making progress, she thought. Next on her list was to find a laundry service for the sheets and towels.

She didn't mind changing the beds, but she couldn't continue to use that outdated and worn-out washer and dryer to launder sheets. She'd have to invest in new machines eventually.

If she did that now, it would take a big chunk out of her savings, and so far this summer, the resort wasn't making enough to buy new stuff. What if something else went wrong, like the plumbing or power or whatever? If such a thing happened, she'd need to have the money to fix that.

But she had to have the washer and dryer…

As she was about to turn the corner, she spotted a medium-sized brick building that looked as if it had been built in the fifties, sporting a sign, Three Corners Community Church.

Elated, she slammed on her brakes and pulled over to the curb. Oh, poor Ol' Winnie. She'd killed the engine, but she paid no attention.

She studied the sign. It also included the pastor's name. Ford Neville.

"Wahoo! Thank you, Lord!" She let the shout roar. She'd attend there Sunday. She couldn't remember when she'd missed meeting the Lord in a worship service for three Sundays in a row. It felt like a starvation diet.

Lord, I can talk to You anywhere and anytime, but I do get a little lonely for Christian companionship.

Sunny sighed happily, and started up the truck again.

Everything would be fine. She just had to trust the Lord to keep her solvent for the year.

Now she was *really* ready to head back to the resort. It wasn't so very confining…

Not confining at all, with Grant down the road. Had it been he who used the dock during the storm? What was he doing there in the middle of the night?

Somehow her evening with Grant loomed as large as the hot, sultry sun. Why, she didn't know.

She bit her lower lip. She shouldn't depend on him so much. Yet she'd been tempted every day to call him. She hadn't intended to do that, become dependent, she wanted to try to take care of things herself.

Grant was a friendly sort, and his invitation to go out tonight was meant only as a friend, because she was new to the area.

Nonetheless, her heart rose in excitement. A date with a good-looking guy with expressive eyes wasn't a bad thing. Not a bad thing at all.

As long as they kept the relationship on a strictly friendship basis…

She just would, that's all. She'd just watch it. And she'd ask Grant what he was doing down at the docks during the storm.

Chapter Six

"Um-hum…" Her gaze flew to the front door as Grant came into the office, and she waved a finger in hello. She was dressed and ready to go. She was also talking long-distance with little Lori.

"Okay, then read about funny-bunny for me, okay? I—"

She clamped the receiver closer to her ear, but watched Grant.

Grant leaned against the door frame, looking cool and ready to roll in clean jeans and a blue polo shirt. He'd left his ball cap off, and his thick hair lay gleaming against his temples. Just that touch of gleaming hair couldn't make him appear younger, could it?

The overwhelming urge to brush her fingers through it swept through her mind; she could actually feel the tickle on her fingers.

She abruptly turned her back, cupping the phone to her mouth. "Listen, sweetie, I have to go now," she muttered into the receiver. "I'll talk to you in a couple of days, okay?"

She swiftly hung the phone in its cradle and turned. She leaned back against the desk, feeling the edge of papers stacked there, the hard edge of the desk cutting into her hips.

"Hi," Grant said, lazy speculation in his gaze.

"Hi, yourself."

"You look nice."

"Thanks." She had on a blue-striped blouse over white knee-length shorts. She wore little makeup—lipstick and one brush with a mascara wand—but the flashy blue earrings that dangled from her ears made up for her lack of cosmetics.

"You ready to go?"

"Just as soon as my new employee comes up. He's working down at the docks at the moment."

"You hired a docks keeper?"

"Well, I hired an assistant. Someone to take care of the docks and the grounds. The office, too, when I need him. I might need him to replace some screens, too, if I can't get a screener or anyone to come out here. Guess we'll have to stumble through that together, if I can't get the professionals. I've decided to replace the screens on all the cabins, after looking at them."

"All of them?"

"Yes. Do you happen to know when the current ones were put on? They look pretty old and ratty. Are they the original screens?"

"Mmm…I don't think so, but maybe. But I'll ask my dad if he knows."

"Say, Grant, you know the cabins pretty well. The beds in some of them are lumpy. I really inspected them last week as I cleaned. How old do you think *they* are?"

"I don't know, but you're right," he said, pursing his mouth as he thought. "Most of the beds are in poor shape. Nathan said something about the mattresses last spring, but—are you going to replace all of them?"

"Yep. I have to. As soon as I can. I'm only surprised customers haven't complained before now. I'm thinking—"

Dell pushed through the door then, jeans wet in splotches. "Okay, Sunny, everything is set."

Dell spotted Grant, his surprised expression one of instant dislike or alarm. Then it was gone. His eyes flickered back to Sunny. "You can take off now. I'll watch the office."

Grant pushed his chin out, his gaze wary. He cleared his throat as if he wanted to say something, but instead he clamped his mouth shut, as though biting down the words. He turned to look out the window.

"Is everything all right down at the docks?" Sunny asked, wondering what Grant was thinking, delaying their leaving. She didn't like the looks the two men had exchanged.

She closed her Bible, which she'd taken to reading in between phone calls during the mornings, the busier time of day. She placed it on the back of the desk.

"Yeah. Got the far lift working smoother," Dell answered. He tucked his thumbs into his back pockets. He didn't look Grant's way again.

Grant stared out the window.

"Okay," she said as she gave in. Nothing was going to be accomplished at the moment.

"It's almost six-thirty. I left sandwich makings for you in the refrigerator if you're hungry, and there's soda there, too." She'd closed her bedroom firmly, tacking a Private sign on it.

"But stick around the office, all right? You're off duty at eight and can close up then. Leave the key... where I told you. If any of the customers want me, I'll be on duty by eight o'clock tomorrow morning."

"Right."

"Right," she answered. Still, she made no movement toward the door.

"Let's get going, shall we?" Grant spoke all too casually as he placed a hand at her elbow and urged her forward. He didn't look at Dell.

Sunny resisted the urge to look back at the younger man. She climbed into Grant's truck determinedly.

They were a mile up the road before Grant, his voice a bit edgy, spoke. "You hired Dell Jackson for this job?"

"Yes." She glanced at him. "Why shouldn't I? He's local and he seems to like the work."

"Mmm...he would."

"What do you mean by that?

"Nothing. It's just that Dell has a reputation."

"Does he? I suppose by that you mean an unlikable one? There's nothing wrong with his work, is there?"

"I guess not."

"Well, I'm glad to get him so soon. I started him on cleaning the flower beds out by the road. He did a thorough job on them. Didn't you notice?"

"Honestly, I didn't." Grant said it as though his mind was elsewhere.

"You don't like Dell?" she accused.

He turned to glance at her, his eyes darkening. "That's not it. Not it at all." He turned back to watch the road. "I don't think he's the best choice you could have made."

Grant questioned her choices? Perhaps he didn't realize that being a charge nurse gave her *some* insights to people. Besides, Dell had been her *only* choice, at the moment. Perhaps later, she'd have a chance at hiring other people, but for now, Dell was the one.

"Why? What's wrong with him?"

"He's irresponsible."

She'd expected that, but not from Grant. How could he know all about the troubled young man? Dell was at the turning point in his life. He might turn into a good worker.

But she didn't like Grant telling her she'd made a poor choice. She could tell *herself* that, thank you.

"That was a long time ago," she said, slightly miffed.

"Only a year. He hasn't changed that much."

"Oh, you think not?" she responded, keeping her heat down with effort, and her hands folded in her lap. "Well, it just so happens that he's just lost his father," she explained the extenuating circumstances. "And Molly, at the employment agency, said he's been without a mother for some time. A child without parents feels…abandoned…and sometimes lost…."

She had, hadn't she?

When her mom died and she went into the foster care system, she was barely twelve. Uncertain, grieving and scared, she'd been placed with a large family who let the kids run wild. No discipline at all. A girl just two years older than she with the unlikely name of Babette had jerked a bright blue sweater of Sunny's from her hand one morning, claiming "It's mine now" regardless of whether it fit her or not. When Sunny protested, Babette hit her hard across the face, telling her to shut up. Stunned, Sunny shrank away.

After that, Babette took every opportunity to treat Sunny cruelly. One night, Babette shoved her violently from bed for no reason other than that another girl was whispering to her.

When Babette threatened Sunny with bodily harm if Sunny didn't give up her dessert, Sunny revolted. Sunny didn't care a hoot about the dessert. She felt outraged at the treatment.

Then she'd made the mistake of complaining. The foster-care mother, overtired and impatient, believed Babette's sweetly given lies, and Sunny was given the job of cleaning the entire kitchen alone as punishment. It was close to midnight before Sunny stumbled to bed that night—only to find her place taken, so she slept the night on the floor with a blanket.

After that Sunny fought back at every opportunity and gained the reputation of being a troublemaker. Off she went to another foster family, which was little better than the first. She'd become a little more accomplished at protecting herself by then, telling a few lies to get along. But she was filling out about then, and a teenage boy who was part of the family tried to take advantage of her maturing body.

Harry tried to corner her every chance he got. Once with Harry's hands all over her was enough. Sunny'd screamed high and wide, causing all the children in the house to run to them, and she'd fought until help came. But nothing was done to correct the boy, and the father in that house only laughed uproariously. That was the first time she'd heard the despised expression "Boys will be boys."

Boys will be boys made her want to scream all over again.

When she was fourteen, she was placed with the Larsons. They were Christian people who believed in following Christ's dictates. And with them, she blossomed. But nearly three years in less than perfect homes had left its mark.

She had a soft spot for any child in trouble. The fact that Dell was already twenty didn't change her mind.

"That shouldn't affect Dell's work—plenty of kids have it hard," she hotly defended.

"Didn't say it would, Sunny. It's just that Dell is no longer a kid, if I'm not mistaken."

"No. No, he's not. Still…losing a parent sure does affect a person's attitude."

Dell *did* need work, but she wasn't defending him for the work. She knew she could make a change in him, given time. First she'd pray for him, then take the steps that the Larsons had with her. Patience and more patience. And talking with him.

She said tentatively, "He's making the best of things."

"Oh, he is, is he? Well, he'll have a lot of proving to do." Grant's chin thrust forward again while his gaze remained straight ahead.

"That's your opinion, I think." Her hands clenched tighter.

"Huh! It isn't only *my* opinion." His sidewards glance didn't convince her.

"Oh? Who else thinks that?"

"Your granddad, for one. Or did."

"Well, Granddad isn't here, is he?"

"He—" His chin got stiffer. His eyes flashed; he looked mad enough to bite nails. "There was a time when your granddad employed him. Dell lasted about a month, then Nathan fired him."

"Oh, yes." She shouldn't explain anything, but she felt the defenses building inside her. "Dell did say something about having been out to Sunshine Acres before. But that's been about two years ago, hasn't it?"

"Yep. Just about the time Nathan and I struck our deal for the land. I was around when Nathan fired him."

So that was it…

"And you think that makes a difference? I take it my granddad didn't care much for Dell?"

"Not with me, there's no difference, and no, he didn't. The kid was totally obnoxious and disrespectful, if you want to know. The day Nathan fired him, he'd been drinking. Wouldn't listen to the old man. Paid the customers little mind. He was a mess."

She was quiet a moment, then said, "I imagine Dell has thought things through since then."

"We can only hope." Grant made the statement strong and doubtful.

Oh, great! If this continued, this would be a *fun* evening. Was it worth quarreling about?

"Let's change the subject."

Grant glanced at her. "Okay by me. I didn't want to talk about Dell all night. What do you want to talk about?"

"Oh, nothing much." She made an effort at calming down. "Your family is scheduled to come down in a few weeks time. They are taking over all the cabins. What's the occasion?"

"Yeah, all the guys. A family reunion, of sorts." Grant was making an effort, too, apparently. "Of the men, anyway. They always come the first week in August. That's how I got acquainted with your granddad, way back when I was a kid. He sometimes went fishing with us. Took us hiking—Gray, my brother, my dad and Uncle Dexter, Uncle Ronnie and the cousins. No one loved the lake area more than Gray or me."

"Ah, I see. Well, that's fine. I'm sure we can entertain the boys."

An irony entered her voice.

"They don't need entertaining, they can do that for themselves," Grant explained, glancing at her. "Dad and Uncle Ronnie have their own boats, so you'll have to be prepared for them. Dad's is a twenty-footer."

"Is that big?"

"For a lake fisherman, it's only so-so. And they'll bring a ton of fishing gear, too."

"Okay, I'll be prepared." She glanced at the sky, clouding over. "Hope it's nice weather for them. That was quite a storm we had the other night."

"Sure was. I had to check the horses when all that thunder was right over us."

"You weren't out on the lake?"

"No." His glance was sharp. "What would I be doing out on the lake on such a night?"

"I don't know. I know someone was. But I couldn't find anyone when I looked." The nerves along her arms tingled, recalling the incident. She was sure there had been someone. "They stopped at our boat docks."

Grant was silent a moment, then he said, "Probably only someone taking shelter from the storm. It happens sometimes. Nothing to worry about."

"I won't. But it's odd that it was almost two in the morning. Awfully late, with the dark and all, to be out, don't you think?"

"Yeah, a little. But it won't happen again, I'm sure."

How could he say that with such certainty?

The man with the craggy face peered from behind a tree, watching the goings-on at Sunshine Acres. He made a path through the brush and trees down the hillside, then walked along beside the lake. A family roasted hot dogs over a small fire at the edge of the water. Thankfully, he saw that he didn't know them.

He avoided them, waving in a friendly manner the way lake folk did, as he made his way back up the hill toward the Sunshine Acres office.

It was getting on toward eight o'clock, so he'd thought it safe to come. It would be dark by nine in July, darker still by nine-thirty.

He heard a noise, spotted Dell sweeping the last of the steps, and dodged behind cabin one.

"Blast…" He cursed under his breath. He waited

with hands behind him against the building. "What is that Dell Jackson doing here," he muttered, brushing his salt-and-pepper hair back. "Blasted female has gone and done it now."

He bit it off, reminding himself it was still light, and people were still active, though the coming night usually caused a settling down. He'd have to confine his activity till full dark.

He wanted to get into the office. There was something there he wanted to see. What she'd done with it.

He wanted to see it all...

Darkness came slowly while his irritation climbed. He wasn't good at waiting.

He tried to shake off their quarrel while he waited until the cabins were all quiet. Dell finally climbed into his rattletrap of a car, and went clattering down the road. As the noise receded, the man remained silent. Around him the sounds of insects and frogs grew. Lightning bugs dotted the dark.

Then he climbed the stairs quickly and silently drifted up to the manager's cabin. A low light had been left on, causing him to grunt in disdain.

He applied his key and slipped through the door.

Chapter Seven

Grant ushered Sunny into the restaurant, feeling a core of rotten clear through his middle. He felt miserable. It was all Dell's fault, he was thinking, looking for someplace to park his anger.

No, it wasn't. His conscience wouldn't let him blame Dell. Not for this tangle.

He hid his sigh as the waitress showed them to a table. He just wasn't used to feeling guilty.

He wished the situation over Nathan's death could all be cleared up. He hated keeping secrets, much less becoming a part of them. It was a good thing she hadn't asked to see Nathan's grave or anything. Yet it was only a matter of time, he thought.

Deception wasn't his thing. It only caused grief.

Besides that, he hadn't counted on Sunny being so…so…

Glancing at her, he decided she wasn't just pretty. She was beautiful in the way a sunny dawn began, with the soft light creeping ahead of the morning, then a burst of light. And looking at her was becoming an addiction. He just wished she wasn't so attractive....

He liked her smile that reminded him of old Nathan, surprising as that was. And he hadn't seen nearly enough of it.

He liked her name, too...Sunny.

Her mother had named her, she'd told him, and for the first time he wondered what *she* was like. He hadn't heard the stories of Johnny's escapades, either. He didn't know near enough of Sunny's background.

When this whole thing began a few months back, he'd asked about the mother. Old Nathan hadn't known a thing about the girl, he'd said. Said his son, Johnny, in his wild, rebellious days of drag-racing and car chases, had known lots of girls. Nathan couldn't know them all, even though Shirley tried to keep track of them.

When Johnny died in a car crash, the heart went out of Shirley. It did Nathan no good, either. Nathan said Shirley had grown quieter through the years. Not bitter, exactly. Simply...without heart.

Grant knew her only as the lady who worked on her flower beds and joked with her customers. He never observed the haunted look in her eyes that Nathan told him about. He'd been too young to notice, he supposed; he was in his teens when she passed away.

Nathan became grumpier along the years without Shirley. Grumpy as all get out, but he wasn't mean with it.

Till now. Grant thought it a little bit mean to keep Sunny in ignorance.

It just wasn't right to keep Sunny in the dark. He'd argued the point till he was blue in the face. But the old man insisted, and since Grant owed so much to him, Grant had gone along. But he didn't like it.

He was tired of the deception now. Why, the old man had nearly blown it the night of the storm. Imagine, creeping about the docks in the middle of strong winds and hot lightning flashes that bounced around the hills like a child's ball. How dangerous…

The storm had scared Sunny. Grant wouldn't have dared going out in it.

"Is this all right?" the waitress asked, pausing at the far table by the window.

"It's fine," replied Sunny. They settled at the small table, and Grant picked up his menu, trying to decide what he wanted to eat. He'd been starved before arriving.

He tried to shake off their quarrel. Over Dell, that just-past-teenage ungrateful scamp. It made him mad to think he'd nearly let his temper get out of hand over Dell Jackson.

He hadn't imagined Sunny was so stubborn.

Only her stubborn, quarrelsome streak was so like her granddad, that it suddenly made him grin.

His irritation vanished. He held the menu higher, to hide behind. All he needed were more questions from her that he couldn't answer.

He bet her stubbornness got her in trouble sometimes, too. The way it did with her granddad.

He cleared his throat, trying to push down his laughter, thinking about families and what part inheritance played, but still amused by the fact she was like her granddad. Better to turn his mind on something else, or he'd lose it altogether.

"Are you hungry?" he said, trying to calm down.

She gave him a suspicious stare. "Sure. Aren't you?"

"Yeah, starved." They ordered, and Grant started talking of the local talent they were about to see. By the time their food came, he no longer thought about Dell.

Yet underneath, he knew he must tell Sunny the truth. Soon. This complicated situation couldn't go on much longer.

On the drive home, he felt fine. Relaxed and good. The show had been funny and light and corny, and he'd chuckled uproariously.

Sunny must have felt it, too. More relaxed than he'd ever seen her, Sunny leaned back comfortably in her seat and chattered of the show on the way home. Imitating the comic who had performed, he started to sing a popular tune, lilting in an exaggerated way till she was bent forward with giggling. His left hand on the wheel, he placed his right hand flat against his chest, bellowing at the top of his lungs.

They hit a bump in the old rough road. The truck bounced hard.

Sunny laughed all the harder.

Then as the laughter died, he dropped his hand to take her fingers. They felt soft against his rough skin, used to doing barn work and taking care of the horses. She'd been a nurse before? That would account for the softness of her hands, he supposed.

He clasped her hand the last mile. He pulled into Sunshine Acres and, letting go her hand to park, he reached to turn off the motor.

He shifted in his seat, leaning back against the door and pulling his knee onto the bench. Her shapely mouth was relaxed as she let out a contented sigh.

Should he kiss her? He wanted to….

She didn't immediately move to get out.

"I appreciate your taking me out, Grant," she said quietly. "I didn't know how much I needed time away from here. I've been on pins and needles trying to learn everything to run this place. Although it's lovely, I must say. The lake, the cabins in this quiet cove and all. I can see why Granddad loved the place."

"We both needed the break, I guess." He reached for her hand again, wanting more than just to hold it. He wanted to feel her soft touch against his face. "I haven't been to one of those shows in a couple of years."

She turned her hand, running her fingers through his.

"Well, tomorrow is Sunday, so I'd better go in. Dell—"

She bit her lip, but he remained silent. When she saw her mention of the youth wouldn't cause another quarrel, she continued. "Dell is going to come and sit in the morning to watch the phone. People don't usually check out till they have to, around noon, but most of them leave sometime in the morning. I think he can take care of it. So I—I've found a church I'd like to attend."

"A church? Where, in town?"

"Yes. Three Corners Community Church. They have

an early service at nine. Would you like to go with me? Or do you…I mean…"

She'd asked him out? He stirred and sat straighter. "Mmm, I guess I've been lazy about finding a church to attend since I've moved here. Though there are a number to choose from. Yes," he drew out the word. "That sounds good to me. Where is it? What time should we leave?"

"About eight-thirty, I think."

"I'll pick you up, okay?"

"That would be great!"

Well, the evening was at an end, he supposed, though he hated to say good night. He watched her lips, telling him about the church, while all he could think about was a good-night kiss.

Evening company had been a little scarce down at the stable, except for Buzz and the old man, and *his* company could be counted on lately only to stir up trouble. He supposed he was getting tired of only male companionship.

Grant got out and went around to help Sunny out of the truck. She switched on the flashlight she'd taken to carrying, and the pooling light made it easier to see as they went to her door.

She paused, gazing into his eyes.

"Thanks again for the outing, Grant. I had a good time."

His stomach said this was it. He'd make his move…

"We'll do it again sometime soon. There's lots to do around the lake, and it's not all connected to water."

"Sounds like a good balance."

"I hadn't thought of it that way, but I guess that's true. I want my riding stable to be one of the other things that this area can offer. It's gaining a good reputation."

"That's good, then. Good night." She suddenly stood on her tiptoes to reach, kissing his cheek. It took him by surprise. "See you in the morning."

Then she was inside and her door was closing. He stood a moment, while his hand went up to cover where her lips had pressed for that brief moment.

Well, thunderation, as Nathan would say... All it was, was a kiss! A little peck on the cheek. He shouldn't make such a big deal of it!

But it had been *her* move, not his.

Sunny woke, stretching fully. She did a few quick bends, touching the floor without bending her knees. It felt good. She felt rested and ready to tackle her day.

She showered, then fumbling in the back of the closet to find something to wear, she dislodged a stack of boxes from the top shelf. They came tumbling down all over the floor.

Kneeling to pick them up, she discovered a number of photo albums. Photo albums?

Her heart began to pound against her chest. These belonged to her grandparents...her family! There would be pictures of her father. And of her grandparents, too.

She glanced at the clock. Eight-fifteen. Fussing at the time, she placed the albums on her bed. She had no time to look at them now. She wanted to spend long hours over them, to study the faces, not to glance hurriedly and not recall what she'd seen. They were her grandparents' precious memories...

Hurriedly, she found a cotton dress in lavender, a favorite from two years before, and slipped it on. Then she found her white sandals.

Tucking her denims into a drawer, she felt thankful her things had arrived from the Larsons.

Thinking of her date with Grant, she found herself grinning. The evening had turned pleasant, in spite of their rough start. Grant kept her laughing, something that had been scarce in her life of late.

But she'd avoid the subject of Dell with Grant. Better to let the boy's work record speak for him.

Grant was very entertaining; he'd sung all the Country and Western tunes they'd heard on their way home. He had her giggling, and they'd said good night on a high note.

She'd kissed him. On the cheek, but still a kiss…

Walking into the office, she opened the front door, and stepped out. She paused to draw a deep breath. As she wandered around the back, she noticed one of the lawn chairs on her deck had been moved. Had Dell been back there?

She strolled down to the docks, noticing that the fishermen from cabin three were up early. They were fishing off the pier. She waved and smiled, but didn't stop.

Returning to the office, she thought of her load of washing. Now that she had Dell, she'd go into town and arrange for a laundry service. The price would be worth the peace of mind that always having clean sheets ready would give her.

Her own clothes could do with a wash, too. She was tired of hand washing, and she had no real place to dry her things. But all that could be done on Monday. She was really getting the hang of this thing, running a resort.

She was hurrying back to the office when tall, skinny Mr. Davis from cabin five hailed her. He wanted an early checkout.

She walked into the office and pulled up his bill. As she did so, she heard male voices, and she glanced out. His buddies stood chatting against a red car: his brother and a second man, a rather husky old guy, with salt-and-pepper hair who stood with his back to her.

The door was open, and she could hear their voices.

She glanced down and counted bills quickly, paying them no mind, hoping she wouldn't be delayed in leaving. She didn't want to be late for the church service.

She hated being late for anything.

"I hope you had a nice stay, Mr. Davis."

"Yeah, it was good. But say, miss, that cabin five, you ought to have the stove checked out. Two burners wouldn't heat right and we could hardly get the fish done last night."

"Oh, I'm so sorry. I'll have it checked before I put someone else in there." The voices outside moved away, and when she glanced outside, the men had gone. She placed the bills in the cash register and closed it. "Thanks for telling me. I am trying to update the cabins as I can."

Dell came in while she stood talking. Behind him came a girl, about fifteen, who looked sulky and resentful.

Dell flashed her an annoyed glance, then led the girl toward the chairs, indicating she was to sit.

"Well, I hope to get down this fall for some deer-hunting," said Mr. Davis. "Good thing you're close to the state reserve. How late are you staying open?"

Privately, Sunny shuddered at the thought of hunting

the sweet animals. But she'd been told the hunting was a necessity for population control.

"Oh, um, until the hunting season is ended, I guess. I'm not too sure when that is. But just call. I'm sure we can accommodate you."

"Okay. Thanks a lot. See you then."

As Mr. Davis left, she noticed him get in beside his brother in the blue van that had been parked for the weekend, and put the car into motion.

Where had the third man gone? And the red car? Wasn't he with them?

Dell brought her mind back to the present.

"I hope you don't mind, but I had to bring my sister. This is Tracy. She won't be a bother." His frown at Tracy said she'd better not be.

"I don't mind, Dell." This child had recently lost her father, too. Her sympathy went out to the child. Of course, she could stay. But would Dell be attentive to his work? "Hi, Tracy. Wouldn't you rather sit down at the docks where you can get some sun? Or on the deck? Perhaps you'd like to swim. There's a diving platform…"

The provisions for swimming were simple. A diving board and a ladder to climb out of the water, on the offside of the docks where it was away from the boats. Sunny had inspected it the first time she'd looked around, but she'd seen it being used only a couple of times. Swimming in the lake was at the customer's own risk.

Perhaps that wasn't such a good idea after all, without anyone to supervise. Some time soon she was going to have to really investigate the swimming facilities.

"Nope," Dell said, relieving Sunny of that worry.

"She has to stay with me. She'll be all right, right here. She brought something to read."

Grant pulled up, and got out of his truck, walking toward the open door. Sunny sighed. He'd objected to Dell being around—what would he say when he found Tracy?

"All right." Keeping her eyes on the door, she said hurriedly, "Well, will you be okay, Tracy?"

The girl glanced up, her face void of expression. "Uh-huh."

"Okay." She grabbed her purse and Bible, waiting on the counter. "I'm going now. I'll be back after church."

She met Grant at the door. He glanced in at the two younger people, but said nothing.

They pulled out, and Sunny resisted looking over her shoulder. Leaving the resort in the hands of a very young man wasn't especially wise, she suspected. But it was only for a few hours. Surely, little could go wrong before she returned.

Grant refused to say a thing. Their quarrel the night before had said it all. She felt blessed that he chose to go to church with her.

He talked of his business, Grant's Retreat. "I am doing a little better this year, and I still have half the summer ahead. In the fall, I'd like to try some Friday-night entertainment. Not only a sunset ride, but a cook-out after, with stories and such. Think it could work?"

"Well, yeah, I'd think it a natural around the lake. Is there anything else like it?"

"I don't think so. I'd have to hire some additional help, too."

They reached the town, and Sunny guided Grant down the right street. They found a place to park, and went in just as the service was about to start. They slipped into a rear pew.

The opening song was one Sunny knew, and her heart lifted with it. She sang the praise with all her might. Beside her, Grant had a creditable baritone, and he added a texture she thought wonderfully fine.

It was so very good to be among believers, she thought; she listened to every word the pastor said in his sermon, and felt renewed as she hadn't been in a long time. Perhaps she'd been working too hard, she thought. Even before she came to the lake, her work schedule was way too heavy.

After the service, a short, balding man Grant knew greeted him enthusiastically, and started talking. Sunny, a few paces into the aisle, stepped aside to let people pass.

"Well, well," said a masculine voice. She turned to spy Jim Lindberg, the Realtor she'd met here her first day. "If it isn't Sunny Merrill. How do you like it out at Sunshine Acres?"

"Why, I like it fine, Mr. Lindberg."

"That's good," he said and nodded. "Please call me Jim. I've been meaning to call you. There is so much to see down here. Are you busy these days?"

"Busy enough." She'd been at Sunshine Acres only a month, but it seemed twice that long. It was nice of Jim to ask. "Haven't had time to think much about it."

"I guess summer is the busy time," he said. "Does your place stay full?"

"Yes, most of the cabins are occupied. Most of the time." She didn't know how Sunshine Acres stacked up against other resorts, but she hoped they were competitive. "Do you know someone who can put new screens on the cabins?

"Hmm, that's good, you have some loyal people. New screens, huh? I can't think of anyone off the top of my head, but I'll ask around. Say, I'd like to take you to lunch some time. How about now? Can you spare the time, by any chance?"

"I'd love to, really," she said, glancing at Grant, still talking, but giving her a steady gaze over the short guy's shoulder. "But I came with Grant, and I have to get back. I'm so sorry."

"Well, maybe later this week," Jim said, noticing her distracted glance. "Maybe lunch on Wednesday? I'd like to have your opinion on a development plan I have. I'll call you Tuesday to firm up plans."

"Certainly. I'll be there."

Grant was frowning at her again. What was his problem? Did he think she wasn't able to take care of herself with a sharp land salesman?

Chapter Eight

"What did Jim Lindberg want?"

They had pulled out of the parking lot and headed toward the road out of town.

"He didn't want anything, he was only being friendly."

"Hmph… The day that Jim Lindberg is only a nice friendly *innocent* guy with no agenda of his own, I'll do a country jig in a pig outfit. He always has a nose for business."

"Why are you so suspicious?" Sunny glanced at him, although his gaze was on the road. "Are you like this with everyone?"

"Suspicious? I'm not normally," he said, tightening his mouth. "Not of everyone."

"Well, it seems that way to me," she said, with a sniff. She felt ruffled again. "First Dell, now Jim Lindberg."

"I promise not to discuss Dell again. But you mark my words, Sunny, Jim Lindberg has his eye on Sunshine

Acres." He said it as though Jim was aiming an arrow right at her heart. "He expects to make a sale with a whopping commission when you're ready."

"What's wrong with that?"

"Nothing." He said it as though he had a whole list of things wrong with that idea. "Nothing at all. Only I'd suggest you find another church to visit. One where Jim Lindberg isn't a member, so you won't see him each week."

Feeling perverse, she answered, "But I liked that church. The people are friendly, and the pastor had a good message. On forgiveness, no less. Didn't you listen?"

"Yes, of course I listened," he said, his exasperation climbing. "It's just that you give that guy an inch, you might as well give him a mile." Then under his breath, "He'll take it anyway."

"An inch or a mile, it makes no difference. You haven't given Jim Lindberg a chance to be simply a friend. Doesn't he deserve your forgiveness in whatever he did or didn't do to deserve your irritation?"

"You are missing my point!"

"What is your point, exactly?"

"He'll harass you to sell."

"Oh, I don't know. I could tell him I won't discuss selling the resort until the year is up. You don't know just how obstinate *I* can be."

"I'm learning," he muttered.

She ignored that. "Then we'll see if he asks me out again."

"He asked you out?"

"Yes." Uh-oh. She shouldn't have told him. "For lunch on Wednesday."

"Oh, great!"

"Now what is that supposed to mean?"

"Not a cotton-pickin' thing, Sunny. Not a cotton-pickin' thing. Let's talk of something else."

Grant set his mouth and drove, hitting the gravel turn-off road too fast, and had to slow down. He was silent and angry, and Sunny wondered how long he would remain that way. When he pulled into Sunshine Acres, he let Sunny slide out of the truck alone.

"Thanks for the ride."

"You're welcome."

"Grant…" They needed to talk about this situation, but there was a car with two men coming in for the week just then. Fishermen, she thought. She had their reservation for a week's stay. "Why don't you come in and have a sandwich?"

"Not this time, Sunny. I've got work to do." Grant put the truck into gear and sped off.

She felt like making a face at him, but caught the eye of her customer just in time. Instead, she disciplined her features and squared her shoulders to greet them.

Dell motioned to where the customers could park, and Sunny turned away, letting her irritation out. Why did Grant find fault with Jim Lindberg?

Sunny slammed into the office, slapping her things down on the counter. Tracy was sprawled over the chair by the desk. She looked up when Sunny came in. It didn't appear the teen had moved all morning. "Hi, Tracy. How's it going?"

"Just fine, ma'am."

Ma'am? That made her smile. When had she become a ma'am?

Sunny went around the counter and pushed her hair back just as the men came inside.

"Ah, Mr. Whitman?" She smiled her welcome. Running the resort was a piece of cake. It wasn't as good as chocolate, but…

She could make that cake chocolate—rich and creamy and delicious. But she'd do it without Grant's advice.

Late Sunday night, Sunny opened the cash drawer to count the money they'd taken in. Mostly, their transactions were done by check or credit card, yet today they'd received cash for a two-night stay in cabin four.

The couple was a young married pair who only wanted a little quiet weekend to themselves. The man had given her two fifties. It wasn't much. Her old cabins couldn't bring in as much as modern resorts that had pools, saunas or other amenities.

She'd have to deposit it though, and she needed to count it. That was another of the things on her to-do list—to open a bank account. She'd neglected that chore, neglected to close her granddad's checking account. That took death certificates.

That reminded her. Where were the death certificates?

She started to count fifties, then startled, looked through all her bills. Hadn't she taken in a fifty-dollar bill last week, too? Yet there was only the two from today.

Shuffling through the twenties and tens, she saw only…twenties and tens. No stray fifty folded with the other bills.

Was she losing her mind? She'd been so busy, she didn't remember putting it anywhere but the cash drawer. On many a morning, she'd been a bit distracted, what with cleaning the cabins, answering phones and keeping the customers happy.

She looked through the drawer again, checking under everything. There were only the tens and twenties. Where could she have put it?

Could someone have taken it? Dell? Or Tracy?

No… She wouldn't go there. Dell and Tracy were having a hard time of it at the moment. She wouldn't give them more trouble. Besides, the cash drawer didn't look as though it had been broken into or jimmied, and Dell didn't have access to it. Surely the money would turn up—if not, she'd just be more careful where she kept it. And be more watchful.

Wandering into her kitchen much later, she noticed the dark shadows of dusk. She should check the docks as she usually did. But she was more tired than usual. It had been a busy day, and she hadn't even taken time for supper.

Out on the deck, she folded herself down into a chair, and stared at the lake. The morning's worship service had filled her with peaceful thoughts, in spite of her quarrel with Grant. Or perhaps because of it? She sighed. She'd simply sit here for the moment and think of the message. Forgiveness…

She wished she had a family to forgive. Would she

have felt that emotion, along with all the love and affection, if she'd had the chance to know them?

She supposed she'd have gone through all of the usual emotional stages.... Even though still a child when her mom died, she had known love and affection, irritation and even anger with her mother—the day-to-day things that families experienced. Even forgiveness.

She drew a long breath and let it out.

Feeling content, she observed the still water, the occasional boat in the distance, and the colors in the dark hills around her in the last of the daylight.

A breeze ruffled the trees over the deck, and she suddenly sat straighter. Did someone want her? She thought she'd heard her name....

She looked around, listening for something.

There was no one calling, and no one around. Yet she'd had the distinct feeling...

Relaxing again, she leaned back in her chair. Imagination again. When would she gain complete familiarity with this place?

Yet, she felt content enough. She was even growing to like lake living.

Except for Grant.

Now why had he come to mind again?

Why did Grant get so uptight with her situation? She had a year—not quite a year, now that she'd been here a few weeks—but she had all that time to worry about selling the place. Jim Lindberg was just helping.

Grant was the problem. He made her so mad, irritation raced up her spine, causing her to squirm in her chair. How dare he criticize her choices? Just because he'd been here in the lake district for a long time didn't give him the right to decide who she should see or entertain. Just because he knew these people…

And she didn't. *That* was the point.

Taking a deliberate breath, she let it out again.

That she didn't know the people well shouldn't matter. What did Grant know, anyway? That Jim Lindberg was an opportunist?

Well, who wasn't? Most people took what came their way, and even worked at making opportunities if they could. Even Grant wanted her land. So what if Jim, a crack real estate salesman, always had his eye on the main chance? In her experience, most males were that way.

Her chair creaked as she shifted. Yeah, most males…

Grant just underestimated her determination to stick to something, that was all. Her perseverance toward a goal. He didn't really know how she'd struggled and worked toward her nursing degree, and these last years, to stay solvent while still helping the Larsons. He just didn't know…

She didn't *really* know these lake people well, either. Not Jim nor Dell, nor…nor anyone, she thought, while Grant's image, his edgy smile, lay full-blown in her mind.

She puckered her mouth. She shouldn't let that smile of his tug at her, but it did.

Just because she liked the way Grant's hair curled against the back of his neck, and the way he suddenly cocked his head at her, listening, and the way his smile edged out when he shouldn't have been laughing…

Sighing, she pushed her thoughts aside. Her feelings must be running high or helter-skelter, she thought in disgust. She should be in control of her feelings, not the other way around.

Laughing at herself, she got up and went into the house. She set out to straighten her small apartment as she ate a cheese sandwich, picking up papers and dusting the furniture. Wouldn't that small table look better over there by that chair? And the low bookcases would serve better under the windows.

She'd work off her mood, she thought. Then shook her head as thoughts of Grant returned.

Grant was too much. He was all male, all right, and evoked responses in her that she didn't know what to do with. She wasn't like her mom, making decisions quickly, loving someone at the drop of an eyelash. Her mom had loved her dad that way, but that wasn't Sunny.

When she finally went to bed at midnight, she found the photo albums. She brushed her fingers over the cover, knowing she had to have time. Time to really study them. She hadn't really forgotten about them, but she felt mentally exhausted.

She'd look at them tomorrow.

Her phone rang early, and she responded quickly. Mondays were always busy.

Dell came in about nine. "Hi, Sunny."

"Hi, Dell. How are you this morning?"

"Fine, I guess. Do you want me to check those loose boards on the dock today?"

"Yes, I think so. I wouldn't want anyone to get hurt."

"Okay, then. I'll get the tools from the garage."

"Dell…how's Tracy? Is she all right?"

"She's okay. She just hates it at Aunt Val's house because she can't have the run of the place. She can't mess around in the kitchen or watch television when she wants to. She misses Dad…and having her own room an' all."

"Yes, but would she like it any better in a foster home? She might be sent anywhere, where there were a dozen kids, or have to share everything," her voice grew hoarse with memories "even her personal clothes. Or the rules there might be much stricter. And she'd be away from you. Would that be any better?"

"Nah, it wouldn't, at that." His eyes brightened. "Thanks, Sunny. I'll point that out to her."

"It's not easy when you lose your parents at too young an age, no matter what."

Dell nodded his agreement. "Yeah, things are tough, but they could be worse, couldn't they?"

"They could, indeed. Hey, Dell, would Tracy be willing to work? Grant needs someone down at Grant's Retreat."

Dell's eyes flashed. "Oh, I don't think Grant would hire Tracy. She don't know anything about horses or stables. Besides, I didn't—that is, we don't get along too well."

"Hmm…well, Tracy might be different, you know."

"Yeah, I guess. I suppose I could suggest it to her. Thanks, Sunny."

The morning grew quiet and Sunny eagerly went to get the photo albums. She'd put off looking at them long enough.

Sitting at the desk in the office, the door open so that she could hear what was going on outside, she opened what looked like the oldest one. She saw snapshots of people in clothes of the 1920s and 1930s. The labels under them read Aunt Pearl and Aunt Hazel and Carl and Clarice and little Timmy and Mother and Father.

She stared at that one a long time. Whose mother and father were they? Were they her ancestors? She had no way of knowing.

Then came World War II pictures, and pictures from the Korean conflict.

Sunny hadn't given any thought to her family serving in the armed forces, or facing violent conflict. Anxiously, she scanned those photos. Labels simply read Casey, or Jess and Dickie in Paris, or About To Ship Out.

Closing that album, she picked the next one.

Ah, this one was more like it. The pictures here were from the 1950s, '60s and '70s. Some of them were even enlarged.

A young woman with a sweet expression and the beginnings of a smile was the first enlarged color snapshot. She had light-brown hair and blue eyes. Cradled in her arms was a baby of about six months.

The label read Shirley and Johnny.

A wave of emotion came swiftly out of the blue, hitting her just under her heart. Sunny bit her lower lip as tears filled her eyes. A baby picture of her dad…and her *grandmother*…

She stared at it long and hard. She didn't know why she felt anything at all. She hadn't heard stories growing up about what this woman was like, what her grandmother liked about this part of the country or how she shopped or what she liked to eat. She only wished she'd known these things.

The phone interrupted her with its insistent ring. She looked up, jerked from her nostalgic mood.

Grant came into the office at the same time, hair brushed to a shine, looking strong and alive.

Rats…he would! She slammed the book shut. What did he want now?

Sunny shoved the album toward the back of the desk so he wouldn't see it, and grabbed the phone. She'd be tied in knots if he saw how much that album affected her.

Grant gave her a little wave as she put the phone to her ear and answered "Sunshine Acres," his grin a welcome sight. It sent a tickling throughout her midsection to know he was no longer annoyed with her.

She placed a hand flat against her stomach, while mouthing "What?" toward Grant.

The screened door came open with a swift, urgent swing. Mr. Perrin, from cabin two, stood there, hands on his hips, looking harried.

"Can you hold, please?" She put her hand over the mouthpiece. "Hi, Mr. Perrin. What can I do for you today?"

"My friend, Jason Ellis," he indicated a short, slender man slumped against a tree outside the cabin, who, even from this distance, looked peaked, "has a raging toothache, and we were wondering if you knew any dentists in town? I hate to take him too far…the pain is bad."

"An emergency? I wonder…" Automatically, her gaze flew to Grant. She didn't know any dentists or doctors in the area. The best she could offer was the area phone book. Instantly, she knew it was something she had to rectify immediately.

"Yeah, I'd say so." Grant stepped forward. "There's a dentist in town just this side of the grocery store. Dr. Kemp. I've been to him once, and he's good. I'll call him, if you like."

"Thanks, thanks a lot." Mr. Perrin looked relieved.

"What's your cell phone number?" Grant asked.

The man gave it, and Grant jotted it down while Sunny quickly took care of the person on the phone and hung up.

"You head on in, and I'll call you when I've made contact with the dental office."

"Are you sure this dentist will take an emergency?"

"Yes, I'm sure. He's a good guy."

As Mr. Perrin went to his cabin, Grant swiftly dialed the number on his cell phone. When he got an answer, he explained the emergency, then listened. "That's fine. Will you phone me when you're through with, um—"

He looked to Sunny to supply the name. "Mr. Ellis."

"When Mr. Ellis is finished?" he said into his phone. "Okay, that's fine."

He clicked his phone off, then dialed Mr. Perrin's number, and reported that the dentist was expecting them, then hung up.

"Whoa!" Sunny brushed her hair behind her ear. "I'm not prepared for a dental emergency." Sunny could kick herself for not familiarizing herself with the medical people in town right away. "I should be. I know what to do for a medical emergency, but dental—"

"You couldn't know, Sunny." Grant was sympathetic.

"Yes, but I should have all the doctors' names, the

hospital, fire and police, all those numbers right by the phone here. What kind of resort is it, not to have those numbers at hand?" She pursed her lips. "It's a neglect on my part. Or my granddad's."

"Nathan probably knows, er, knew those numbers by heart, Sunny. He probably didn't think to place them by the phone."

"I guess not. But I should've known better. I'll type them up and have them in place by tonight, *that* you can count on. You can advise me on which doctors are most likely to take emergencies…"

She brushed her hair behind her ear a second time. "Now, why did you stop by?"

Chapter Nine

Sunny was a tad upset. She watched out the window as Mr. Perrin and Mr. Ellis drove away while she did nothing. She'd been trained to do *something* in an emergency, and she felt helpless now.

"I was bored, and I wanted a sandwich," Grant said with a grin, leaning back against the counter. He crossed his ankles nonchalantly.

She turned and raised a brow. She placed a hand on her hip and refused to respond to his compelling grin. She *really* believed that one. She regarded him with a jaundiced eye.

"Mmm..."

"Okay, okay," he conceded. He dropped his arms to his sides and stood away from the counter. "I wanted to talk to you. To apologize for my behavior on Sunday. I was way off base."

"You were," she said in agreement. She walked back to the desk.

"Churlish and childish."

"You said it, I didn't." She began to straighten the desk, which was already neat. She'd created a place for everything, and everything was in its place.

"Look, Sunny, I wouldn't blame you if you wanted to feed me to the fish. I admitted I was in the wrong. Now cut me some slack, please?"

Giving in, she stopped what she was doing, and stared at him, hiding her sigh. He gave her a pleading gaze, one that stirred her to forgiveness. Finally, she said softly, "Come on, I'll make you a tuna sandwich."

Behind her, Grant let out his breath. Sunny didn't think she was an easy pushover, but she could be wrong. He was altogether too…too… What was it about Grant that caused her always to give in?

She led the way into the apartment, and went to the cupboards. She got out a bowl and a can of tuna.

Grant took a kitchen chair and watched her. She felt his gaze on everything she did, each movement. It made her feel warm all over, but she refused to let it interfere with making tuna salad.

"It's almost August," he said out of the blue. The smell of tuna filled the air, then as she opened the jar, the odor of pickle relish. She cracked the hard-cooked egg she'd boiled that morning.

"Uh-huh?"

"You have my folks' reservation?"

"Yeah, somewhere." She added mayonnaise, salt and pepper, and stirred. "Do you want lettuce?"

She knew right where the reservation lay, stacked with three others. She knew how many in the party, too.

She knew this was the twelfth season the family had been at Sunshine Acres for a week in August.

Twelve... What was she doing twelve years ago? That was a few years after she lost her mother.

She pushed the thought aside. It was no use thinking of the "what ifs" in life.

"They'll be down bright and early on Sunday and Monday," he reminded.

"Good, good. That's just fine. We'll be ready. Lettuce?" she asked again, twisting at her waist and glancing at him over her shoulder.

His eyes narrowed. "Sure, why not? Are you really prepared for an influx of men?"

"A good many of my customers are men," she said in a matter-of-fact tone. "What's so different about your family?"

"Not much. They're just your ordinary uncles and cousins, and my father and my two brothers, Gray and Linc. A little crude sometimes, a little off-color when with all men, you know. My sister, Ginny, stays home with Mom, and they go on a live theater spree. They see every production in Kansas City."

Sunny smiled. "That's nice."

Nice, indeed. She said it with a lightness she almost felt; she'd always wanted to be part of a large family— the fairy-tale kind with perfect people. She knew only too well what the nightmare kind was about.

The Larsons had been her blessing, she reminded herself, and she thanked God for them. She should be grateful for what she had.

Truth to tell, she didn't much trust in fairy tales. Her

only real trust was in God and His Son. How else could she explain this sudden blessing of owning a resort? Still, she muttered, "Wish I could join them."

Grant continued as though he hadn't heard her.

"But the men have this tradition of coming down here. They've stayed at Sunshine Acres the first week in August for ages. They can get a little rowdy at times, though. Nothing out of hand, but—"

"Why, what do they do?"

"Oh, nothing much. They fish most days and go boating. Go swimming and play games. Eat and slob about the place. You'll have a major cleanup when they leave."

His voice was heavy on the "major."

She stilled a moment. "Are they drinkers?"

"Uh…not much. Uncle Clint and his boys drink a little, but we don't do much of it because of the children. But Uncle Tab doesn't touch the stuff."

"Children?" Her heart lightened. "Oh, I thought you were talking of all adults. Why, that's no problem." She popped a potato chip into her mouth, then offered the bag toward him. "Children, huh? I'll have to think of something special for them."

"Yes, I've got a couple of small cousins." He reached into the bag and took a handful of chips. "Connor is eight or nine, and Josh is eleven, I think. It's Connor's first time down with the men. They think they're big stuff, getting to come. Rites of passage and all that stuff. The biggest thing in their life is they can stay up till all hours."

"I think I'll get out the badminton set I found in the garage and look at it." Her mind raced as she set the sandwiches on plates, and opened the refrigerator, getting out two soft drinks.

What else could she do to make Sunshine Acres pleasant for little boys? "Let's go out on the deck, hmm?"

He picked up a plate, and opened the slider. Allowing her to go first, he then sat down on the wooden stairs. She chose a chair, resting her head on the back, then asked, "Would you like to ask God's blessing this time, Grant?"

The request startled him, she could tell that. But ask him she had, and he could always refuse. She wondered if he'd ever prayed aloud before.

Grant thought about it for two full seconds, his expression one of surprise. Certainly, on this issue he felt shy in front of her. Although why it should make him so was a puzzle.

He silently joined the prayers of church leaders on a Sunday morning—that wasn't anything he shied away from—and he'd prayed a heaping bunch before taking on Grant's Retreat—but to pray aloud?

Yet as he thought about it, the request wasn't beyond what he could give.

"Okay…" he found himself saying. He closed his eyes. "Father, we ask your blessing on this food. And on this day. We praise You for giving it. We pray You will bless the weeks coming, and guide us in…in the…the particular activities that we're involved in. Sunny's efforts at running this resort, and my rides and my stable. Thanks for listening, Lord. In Your name, Amen."

As she picked up her sandwich, Sunny's gaze was

thoughtful. "Thanks for that, Grant. You really meant it, didn't you?"

"Yeah…I guess I did." He felt his neck get hot, and dropped his eyes. He couldn't look at her, couldn't tell if she was pleased. Yet he knew it wasn't she that he was trying to please; it truly was the Lord. "Never prayed out loud before." His voice was husky. "But I guess if the Almighty doesn't mind, it's okay."

"Um," he changed the subject quickly "about the badminton. I don't think it's in good shape. It hasn't been out in a long time."

He picked up his sandwich and munched.

"Then I'll just have to get a new one, don't you think?" Sunny picked up her own sandwich. "I could set it up by the road. It's almost flat there. It needs some clearing. I'll have Dell go over the area for rocks."

"That's a good idea. And with Connor and Josh in attendance, it'll get used, I'm sure. You can send the crowd over to my place for a horseback ride one morning, too. I'm eager for my brothers to see Grant's Retreat. They…they believe in me and all, but I'd like for them to see it."

"Haven't they been down?" She asked the question incredulously. He glanced at her, noting her thoughtful gaze.

"Mom and Dad have been, but my brothers and my sis haven't. They've been busy. Linc's still in high school, Ginny's in college, and the courts take all of Gray's time."

"That's too bad," she murmured.

"Oh, they've seen it in the building stage, and approved of Buzz, my sometimes handyman, sometimes cook, but the Retreat wasn't complete last year when they were down. I've got the trail extended over the hill now, and I have enough mounts for all of 'em if I take the crowd in shifts. I think they'll like the longer ride."

He thought a bit. "Might take two mornings to give the whole crowd a ride. But I'll manage. I can do breakfast for them, too, outside with a campfire. They'd like the camp-out, and it would be a good run to see if I could handle it with customers. Buzz makes great biscuits, and I can handle the eggs."

"Could you really cook out for that many?" Sunny asked.

"Sure, why not? If I hope to do Friday- or Saturday-night rides, with supper, I'd better learn to handle it."

"Okay, that works. What else?"

"I guess I could put in a horseshoe lot, too. I know the older guys would go for it."

"Horseshoes? I haven't seen horseshoes in a dog's age. Don't you need a perfectly flat place for it?"

"Yeah. There's a spot for it down a ways from the barn." He laughed. "It's a cinch we have plenty of horse shoes."

"Oh." She cocked her head to one side, a smile hovering. "I hadn't thought of that. You have to have shoes for your horses, hmm?"

"Yep. A farrier comes over from his place in Kansas when I need him."

"A farrier?" Her forehead wrinkled.

"That's a guy who shoes horses."

"Oh, I learned something new. Must be quite a place. I'll have to come see it sometime."

He glanced at her, imagining her at his place, with

its big red barn and stables, and tiny three-bedroom house. It seemed funny she'd been here all these weeks and yet not been to his place. In spite of the complications…

"Wish you would. Grant's Retreat isn't much, yet. But I intend it to be larger some day. I'm at the end of the road and the road won't go beyond me. Your grand-dad helped me design it, and he intended…" He caught his words before they could be uttered, not desiring to start an argument. "Well, never mind. Why don't you come along on a ride, Sunny? See it for yourself?"

"Invite me."

"I do," he said with a positive air. "I will," he added with growing enthusiasm. His blue eyes flashed with a quick, glowing satisfaction. "Dell can watch Sunshine Acres for a morning. We can do it next week. That way, I…um…I'll clear it."

"Okay. I'll come."

He chuckled. "I'll feed you for a change. Want to come for breakfast?"

"Well, it's done. I invited her," Grant said much later in the day as he brushed a roan mare, Lazy Daisy, in the corral beside the barn. The mare had picked up a peb-ble in her foot the day before, and he wanted to be sure she was ready for tomorrow's ride.

Five people for tomorrow. That was good, especially after the nine yesterday. Only three today, though. He had to increase his business before next year, or supple-ment it some way.

He glanced up to the house. It wasn't big, only three

tiny bedrooms, but it had a huge kitchen. It had been designed so that a second phase could be added later. He hoped that would happen by another year.

Never mind that. Grant's Retreat was doing pretty well for only being open a year. He had to be satisfied with that, and wait patiently for things to improve.

The clean odors hit his nostrils—horse and grass and hay—all so different from the resort up the road. Life seemed simpler at Grant's Retreat.

How he'd got roped into all this complicated secrecy was beyond him. He wished his riding date with Sunny was just that. A simple date.

He liked Sunny… He liked her a lot. Maybe too much.

The old man chuckled. He was next to Grant at the corral fence, brushing a black mare. The horses would be turned out to pasture afterwards. "Told ya you could do it, didn't I?"

Grant didn't feel like laughing.

"Yeah, you told me. But what is that going to prove?" He'd felt lower than low about making up with Sunny on the old man's say-so. He felt like a spy. He should have made up with her on his own.

He'd intended to—why hadn't he?

But the old man'd pushed and nagged until Grant had given in, and then Grant was as uncomfortable as if the pebble had been found under *his* skin. Grant promised to remain silent about Jim Lindberg from now on, too, though it stuck in his craw.

And Dell, for crying out loud. Though he'd have to admit, the boy had worked surprisingly hard for Sunny.

He continued his brushing, giving the roan an extra five minutes. Lazy Daisy could use the attention.

Well, Sunny was a strong-minded female. *That* he'd discovered right quick. And continued to discover. Why her smile affected him so, he didn't know, but he'd like to find out.

He thought of the way it curved, making an impression into the cheek. Like her granddad's. Oh, yeah! It affected him all right. And he'd pay for it with heartache if he wasn't careful.

Sunny was going to visit Grant's Retreat one day soon, and despite his annoyance with the old man, his expectation ran unreasonably high. Would she like it? Find it interesting? Would she want to know more, approve of his future plans for the place? Like a little kid, he wanted to show off his prize.

He'd pay for this deception, too. But Nathan wanted it. He only wished his acquaintance with Sunny was a natural one.

After Grant got started with his apology, he'd found Sunny easy to talk to and he'd spilled out a lot about himself. Of his plans for Grant's Retreat. And about his family.

It still felt too much like deception.

Her grandfather answered, "Nothin', I guess. It's not going to prove a thing. Just give me a chance to find out how she knew to contact me, who told her. If I find out it's that Frankie fellow, I'll wring his neck before I turn him over to the authorities."

Grant felt his friend's outrage across the yard. He couldn't entirely blame him.

"You just have to see how she's running the resort, you mean?" Grant said, hoping to soothe Nathan's feelings. "Know if she's got the personality for it? Is she competent?"

"Somethin' like that, of course. Just gives me a chance to know more of what she's really like. If she's been conniving with that Frankie. Or if she's mixed up with Frankie Brewster at all. If her personality is anything like Johnny's, too easy, and subject to the alcohol, I won't count on more. I just— He broke his mother's heart, you know, and I—I—" The older man broke off his words as his eyes welled up.

"All right," Grant said, gently patting the old man's shoulder. He led the mare toward the gate, letting her into the pasture.

"Gotta know if she's steady…" Nathan followed, leading the black mare.

"So be it," Grant said, hiding his sigh while watching the two horses immediately start to crop grass. "But I'm telling you, she'll find you out if you keep prowling about the resort. She's no dummy. We can't keep this up much longer. I don't *want* to keep it up."

He couldn't keep up the deception…

He felt like a louse.

"Just a little while longer, Grant." Nathan's usual commanding voice held a begging quality. Grant knew the old man's emotion behind it. His friend had to do things his way, this once. "Till just after your folks are here. See how she handles that, what her strengths are. I'll know then if I can trust her. And I'll have more time to find out if she knew of Shirley and me all along."

Grant knew enough of Sunny now. She hadn't known. And what did it matter, after all? Kids and grandkids seldom followed your wishes in life. They chose their own way.

But after she knew of this fiasco, would she ever trust *him* again?

Chapter Ten

Sunny had to do laundry. She was wearing her last clean pair of underpants, and all her casual clothes were dirty. She could always wash a few things out by hand, which she'd been doing, but if she didn't get to the laundry today, she'd be forced to wear dressy clothes around the resort. Or her nurse's uniform.

That image made her laugh. She'd scare the customers, she thought. Then she bit her lip in thought. She could go without a bra by wearing her bathing suit top, but she didn't like to do that while working in the office. Besides, she hadn't worn her old bathing suit much. Just once last year, she thought. Who had time to swim?

She had to do a major amount of laundry.

Luckily, Dell was due to be here any moment.

Packing her overflowing basket, she stuffed soap and bleach into the side. The phone rang, and she went into the office to pick it up.

"Sunshine Acres."

"Sunny?"

"Yeah, Dell, I'm here. You're supposed to be here right now. What's the matter? Where are you?"

"I'm in town. I've had an accident. I'll be a little late."

"Are you all right?" Her mind leaped to all sorts of possibilities. Did he need to see a doctor? Was he hurt? Was he making an excuse?

"Yeah." He sounded uncertain, a bit dispirited. "But I don't have a car."

"You don't?" Her heart slowed. If that was all… "Where are you?"

"I'm—I'm, uh, at the Breadbasket Restaurant?"

"Where is that?"

Dell told her.

"I'll be there as soon as I can. Don't leave till I get there."

"All right."

With swift movements, she loaded her basket in the big truck, made sure the answering machine was on, locked her door and tacked a note on it, all the while worrying whether Dell was telling her the truth, that he *was* all right.

If he needed medical attention, she'd see to it.

When she turned around to get into Ol' Winnie, a customer was standing there. "Oh…may I help you?" She searched her memory for his name. "Mr. Egan?"

"Uh-huh. How are you?

"I'm just dandy. What can I do for you?"

"I called a parasailing company to come here about eleven o'clock this morning. They need permission to put in at your docks. That's okay, isn't it?"

"Oh, sure. But are you sure they want to come this far? We're a bit far away from the commercial crowd."

"No, no. They said they'd come, they don't mind. It'll cost extra, but I'm willing to pay it."

"Okay." She nodded, her mind racing to Dell and thinking of the resort, too. She supposed it would be all right. They wouldn't need her. "I'm leaving the office unattended for the morning. But I don't expect you'll have any trouble. Have fun with the parasailing."

He grinned. "I plan to. My son's going, too."

Nodding, she waved goodbye.

She climbed into the truck, waved goodbye again with a smile to show everything was fine, and started the motor. She looked over her shoulder to back out, blessing the quiet road. She didn't have to worry about oncoming traffic—only Grant was down the road beyond her. Thank God, too, she could trust her transportation. In Minneapolis, she'd never have dreamed of owning a good-running truck, but on her rough road, she was glad she had it.

As soon as she hit hard tarmac, she pushed the gas pedal. When she hit town, she slowed Ol' Winnie and watched the street signs until she found the one she wanted. She spotted the restaurant across the street, and at the corner she made a U turn.

She parked two vehicles down on the street and slid out, entering the restaurant at her speedy nurse's walk. She stood a moment in the entrance, hoping she'd come to the right place. Then in a back booth, she spotted Dell and Tracy, looking tired and miserable, sad and dejected. Tracy was tucked defensively against the wall while Dell sat opposite.

Poor kids. She recognized their expressions.

Walking swiftly, she approached them. Dell sat slumped in the booth, his head in his hand, his elbow on the table. He had a darkening bruise on his cheek, his eye was puffy, and the shoulder of his T-shirt was torn.

Sunny stood and stared at him, then thrust out her chin. "That's no accident, I'm thinking. What happened?"

"Nothing," Dell said. His tongue went round inside his mouth as though tasting blood.

"Oh, yes, it is. It's something, all right," she insisted. She leaned toward him and hardened her voice. "I've been trained to spot lies, you know, and I know kids, and I can see you've had some sort of altercation. Don't lie now. Tell me what happened. And who with?"

Dell glanced at her, his mouth set. He took his hand down, sank lower in the booth and crossed his arms. But he said nothing.

"Are you going to tell me about it or am I going to have to drag it out of you? I can, you know. I'm as stubborn as all get out. Who did you get into a fight with?"

Tracy spoke up then, slowly, her eyes full of apprehension and her voice thin. "Uncle Clyde. He kicked Dell out of the house for no other reason than that he…he didn't come home on time and…smarted off. He didn't make curfew last night."

Sunny was silent a moment, recalling the times when Jessica and Mark faced a similar crisis. When about seventeen, once she'd been late from work; she'd missed her bus home. There was no telephone nearby, and she was too scared to find a restaurant or public place from which to call. That she hadn't called had them worried.

"Where were you that you didn't make curfew?"

"Working."

Her brows shot up. "Working? A second job? Where?"

"At the pool hall downtown. It doesn't close till midnight, and I put in evenings there, cleaning up, waiting tables. Whatever."

"I thought you had to be twenty-one to work in a pool hall." She felt a bit of outrage. "Do they serve…never mind, of course they do."

Again, Dell silently stared at the table in front of him. No doubt he'd served anything they'd wanted him to serve. And he hadn't called home to tell his aunt and uncle he would be late.

Tracy spoke as she pushed her brown hair out of her eyes. "He told them he was twenty-one."

"Uh-huh." That figured. "And what did your Uncle Clyde say to that?"

"Uncle Clyde came in and made trouble, but he did it to humiliate Dell," said Tracy, defending her brother. Her chin thrust out. "Not 'cause he cared at all. He made a big thing of it, and threatened the manager if he let Dell work there again. The dirty jerk."

"And you got fired?"

"Yeah," mumbled Dell.

Thank God for small favors, Sunny thought. "What happened then?"

He looked up at last, sporting a defiant glare. "I took a swing at Clyde, the stinking pig. A real swing, and landed him a good one."

"Gave him a black eye," muttered Tracy. It didn't seem to Sunny that Tracy was altogether sorry.

"He had it coming," said Dell, a tiny bit of pride showing "For getting me fired. Can't stand the jerk. Pick, pick, pick. Nag, nag, nag. Takes most of my pay, and I have trouble making my car payments."

He looked down at his fists. "Makes Tracy miserable, too."

"Shh, Dell…"

So that was the way it was. Sunny took a deep breath.

"I'm not going to defend the slimeball, Tracy."

"But, Dell, we have to *live* with him. Can't you just, you know, find a way to—to make him happy?" Tracy pleaded.

"No, I can't, Tracy. You know how it is. The guy was just looking for an excuse to get me out of his house. Clyde wants you, all right. But he didn't want me in the first place. Only Aunt Val was shamed into keeping us. Now I'll have to find another place to stay. A room somewhere. And you'll be left to that no-good—"

"Please, Dell, don't talk that way," Tracy begged. "Don't leave me there, I can't stay without you there."

"I can't take you with me, Tracy," Dell's voice rose in desperation, his eyes pleading with her. "I don't have no place to take you."

"You can stay with me." Sunny said it without a prior plan or thought in her head, but she spoke positively. "You can have one of the cabins."

Two young faces swung to stare at her, open-mouthed. As what Sunny said took root in her mind, Tracy's face lit up like a Christmas tree full of lights. "You—you mean it? We can have one of the cabins?"

Dell's face was doubtful. "What are you saying, Sunny?" Dell slowly sat up, his face looking suddenly very young. "You can't do that. It means you'll be giving up part of your income."

"You let me worry about that. I can provide you with a place to stay, if you want it. At least for this next year."

Pushing her hair back, she placed her hand on her hip, then said more softly, "Shoot, I don't know what the winter will be like, but you'd be company for me. My year… Never mind."

She straightened again. "You can work for the rent and find another job here in town. It'll even out." She lowered one eyebrow at Dell. "A respectable job, mind you, with no serving of alcohol until you turn twenty-one. And Tracy will finish high school. You can work on Saturdays, too, Tracy."

"That would be super!" Tracy said. "But my aunt…"

"We'll have to square the living arrangements with your aunt. Will she let you go?"

"I don't know. I think so," said Tracy.

"Yeah," said Dell. He pushed out his lip. "You bet, with Clyde griping all the time."

"And with Social Services, I think. But if you're living out at the resort, and working—" Sunny stared steadily at Dell "—then there shouldn't be a problem. That way you can stay together."

"Oh, wow!" Tracy grinned, her smile as bright as the morning sun.

"I'll have to get another job," Dell mused.

"Yep," Sunny was firm. "And soon. No lazy bones allowed at my place. I'm not supporting the two of you.

I'm only giving you a fair *temporary* shake. You'll have to support yourself."

"I'll get something." Dell sat straighter, his eyes starting to shine.

"I think the faster we talk to your aunt, the faster we'll have this thing settled," said Sunny.

"Um, one problem." Dell looked worried.

"What is that?"

"Clyde took my car."

"He what? How could he take your car?"

"He sneaked it away, and I don't know where he put it. He said it was for all the headache I put him through."

"Well, if the car belongs to you, then I expect we can get it back." She thought of contacting the sheriff, yet she hoped it wouldn't come to that. "It does belong to you, doesn't it?

"Yeah, it's mine all right. I worked for it, and I've got the ownership papers."

"All right then. Come on, we'll see your aunt right away."

Sunny put the matter of the resort out of her mind. The answering machine would take the calls. If her customers wanted something from her, they'd just have to wait. This was more important.

It was after two when she got back to the resort. She slid tiredly out of the truck, the hot sunshine beating down on her head. She hitched her purse to her shoulder, hauled her laundry basket out of the truck bed, and welcomed the shade of the trees as she carried it to her cabin. She set the basket down to unlock the door.

The phone was ringing.

She sighed and hurried to turn the key. She hadn't had lunch, and she hadn't had time to go to the grocery store, and her laundry was clean but not folded.

And Dell and Tracy would be there by supper time.

"Hello. Sunshine Acres," she answered, the laundry basket at her feet. She grabbed a tissue and swiped her sweaty forehead. "Yes…next week? I'm sorry, I don't have anything free next week. But…the week after next, I have a cabin free."

Taking the phone, she dragged the line to the far wall to check the temperature on the window unit. It was set for seventy-two, but it didn't feel cool enough. "Sure. Just call when you want to make a reservation. Thank you for thinking of Sunshine Acres."

She hung up, saw there were two calls on the answering machine, but decided the return calls could wait. She took the laundry into the bedroom and dumped it on her bed.

What had she taken on? She wasn't following Jessica and Mark Larson's pattern, was she?

Dell and Tracy's aunt had been at work when they skulked into the house. Clyde didn't work much, Dell whispered as they entered the ranch-style house. They woke Clyde, a big hulking dark-headed man, sleeping in his lounge chair. He sported a dark bruise under his eye, evidence of Dell's slugging fist.

The kids said as little as they could when they went in, but made it clear that they were leaving, and went immediately to pack.

Sunny stood just inside the door. Tracy introduced her merely as a friend and employer.

From his lounge chair, tipped back for comfort, Clyde clutched his beer can over his protruding belly and gave a cruel laugh. He boldly gave Sunny a once-over. "I suppose you're gonna take them on?"

She stiffened her spine against the insult.

"Not at all. They plan to make it on their own," she answered. *Lord, I sincerely hope they can. Please give the kids what they need.* "But Dell really needs his car."

"He ain't gettin' his car back." Clyde took a sip of his beer.

"I imagine the County Sheriff will have something to say to that," Sunny said, holding her head high, returning stare for stare.

Clyde twisted his face into an expression of contempt. "That's the way it is, huh?" he said angrily. "All right, but those kids're never coming back here, you know. I've had all I can stomach of 'em."

Dell heard his uncle's contemptuous remarks while walking through the living room carrying a clock radio and a wastepaper basket filled to the top with CD player, CDs, and socks. He stopped to glare at Clyde.

"As *if!* I wouldn't set foot here ever again for a million bucks. And if you don't give me back my car, you be watching your own car… For flats. Or cracked windshields or—"

"Dell," Sunny whispered. All these kids needed was to be caught in a vicious family feud. It wouldn't be good for her, either. Besides, it would be better and eas-

ier if Dell left this all completely behind him to get on
with his life.

Clyde let out a roaring cackle. He half left his chair,
giving Sunny heart palpitations thinking he was going
to start a fight. But instead, he dug into his pocket,
over his fat belly, and finding the car keys, threw them
scornfully across the room. They bounced off Dell's
shoulder.

"Take the stupid car. If that'll get rid of you, then fine.
It's parked behind the grocery store. Don't want nothing more to do with you."

"That's just fine with me, you old—"

"Dell!" Tracy placed her hand on his arm.

Dell swirled on his heel and stormed out, then came
back for his clothes stuffed in a pillow case. Tracy came
dragging another two pillowcases behind her. She
stopped long enough to flash Clyde a defiant glance.
"I'll call Aunt Val."

"Don't bother. I'll tell her."

Tracy tightened her lips against saying another word.
They turned and left, and Sunny felt relieved.

"I will, though. He can't stop me," Tracy said. Sunny
guessed there were tears in her eyes. Dell took her pillowcases and swung them into the truck bed.

"We're through here," Dell crowed.

Sunny sighed now, thinking it through. She'd
driven them to pick up Dell's car, then gone on to the
laundromat.

Never mind. It would all work out. It had to. She'd
pray about it. *Lord, You know all about it…*

She checked the air-conditioning once more. It didn't seem to be cooling the room properly. She left it.

She slapped together a peanut butter and jelly sandwich, took a bottle of water from the refrigerator, and despite the heat, decided to take a break down by the lake.

Chapter Eleven

Sunny folded herself down on the edge of her property near the lake where the weeds began. It smelled of grasses and lake water and fresh air. A fish jumped out in the lake, creating lazy circles in the water. She sat a moment, letting the peace of the place surround her.

The Lord's Creation staggered her. Oh, she knew this lake had been created by mankind, but the beauty…she was inclined to believe that was the Lord's.

She hadn't seen much of the world, but could anything be prettier than this vista? Across the cove were hills in various shades of green. The earth there plunged to the water from a high point, over sheer rock creating a cliff. Could the deserts, mountains, gorges or canyons be any better? Or prettier? She recognized that each held its own beauty, but this place….

She could see why her grandparents had loved it.

A motor boat came in to the dock; an elderly couple from cabin six got out and lingered a time, but finally started up the concrete steps toward their cabin. Spotting her, they waved merrily.

She waved back with a smile, then bowed her head, earnestly thanking God for her lunch. She was so grateful for her life; it could have turned out so differently.

Sinking her mouth into peanut butter and bread, she heard steps behind her. Turning, she saw Grant.

"Hi."

"Hi." She pushed peanut butter to the corner of her mouth to speak. She hadn't seen him in a couple of days. They still hadn't set a date for her to ride. "What are you up to?"

"Nothing much." He sank down beside her. "I've been busy with the horses. And customers. Took out two parties yesterday," he remarked with pride. "You just now eating lunch?"

"Mmm-hmm…I was busy in town. Want a bite?" She held out her untouched half, peanut butter oozing. It was her comfort food.

He glanced at it, but said, "Nah, I had lunch."

"How's business?" She swallowed, took a swallow of the ice water she had in a plastic glass, and picked up her other sandwich half.

"I've got two morning rides lined up for Saturday, and one for the afternoon. If my summer rides keep up for one more month, I'll be okay this year. Better than last year, anyway. After that, I'll make a profit."

"Mmm…that's good, isn't it? That means your business is building."

"Yep. Want to go for a boat ride?" Grant's gaze was warmly inviting.

A soothing boat ride… She wished she could—to find more peace, to feel the breeze against her skin. She glanced back up to her office. She'd been out all day.

"Maybe later. I don't think I should leave the office again just now. Besides, I've got work to do."

"Oh, that's always there." His gaze followed hers, back over his shoulder, then coaxed, "Come on, it would do you good. Cool you off."

"Yes, it sounds wonderful, but I shouldn't, not just yet. Thanks anyway. When are you going to give me that ride we talked about?"

Did he hesitate?

He hastily said, "How about tomorrow? I have a party of four coming at nine. You could do it then."

At nine, hmm? "Maybe. Let me see how this afternoon shapes up. I'll let you know this evening."

"Okay. I'll see you then." He rose and strolled down to the docks. He fiddled around at his boat awhile, then put-putted away, back toward his land. Sunny stared longingly for a moment, took a deep breath, then briskly picked up her lunch leavings.

Time to get back to work. The elderly couple was leaving tomorrow, and two more customers would arrive. Customers in cabins five and two were staying until Monday. That left cabin one for Dell and Tracy.

She'd have to check cabin one again if the kids were to have it, she thought as she sauntered back up to the office. She wished she could make the cabin a little less impersonal for them, but her own cabin wasn't in any position to be called "Sunny's apartment," was it? It was only the office. All the cabins were impersonal and out of date.

That was something to think about, she mused. If she were to stay the whole year, shouldn't she have some personal items about? More than just her clothes? Make the apartment more hers?

Shouldn't she do some updating for all of the cabins? She knew the beds needed new mattresses, and the screens needed redone. She hadn't pursued that.

She hadn't been thinking of this place as her home, she mused. She'd been thinking of it as temporary living quarters. Even her clothes were temporarily hung or stuffed in that small chest of drawers. She'd been living as though she'd move tomorrow.

But if she'd learned anything in her years of passing from family to family, it was to have something of her own, something no one could take away from her in place. She should have something now.

Out of the blue, she wanted to talk to Jessica Larson. And little Lori, too. She'd been too busy to talk with them all week, and she missed them. This life was made up of meeting people only to see them go the next week.

Was that why she'd been so dependent on Grant? Or, more to the point, why she'd held him at arm's length?

She'd like to believe that she didn't find him so attractive, but his quick easy grin seemed to send her nerves into a free-for-all.

Pushing her thoughts to the back of her mind, she went inside. The office was quiet now, so she settled into the office chair and dialed the long-distance number. Talking to her old friend and mentor would settle her nerves.

"Hi, honey." She could hear weariness in Jessica's voice.

"Hi, Jessica. I was feeling a little homesick, I guess. How are you? And Lori?

They chatted about ten minutes, then she saw Dell and Tracy through the window as they parked their old car.

"Okay, I have to go," she said, watching the two haul themselves wearily out of the car. Yet there was an air of excitement about them. "I'll call again in a couple of days."

"Oh, Sunny, before you go, Dr. Jensen's office called."

"They did? What did they want? When?"

"Yesterday, and they wanted your phone number. I didn't give it to them. I thought you should call them."

"Yeah, I'll call them. Don't worry, Jessica."

But it was something, Sunny thought as she hung up. She bit her lip. She'd taken a leave of absence, not knowing when she left exactly what she faced here in Missouri. But she couldn't ask them to hold her job for a whole year. She'd have to resign.

Letting go of her job gave her a funny feeling. She wanted to clutch at it, solid and steady. She'd worked so hard for the position.

Never mind that. She'd call tomorrow—it was the only thing she could do.

She walked out of the office to see about the kids.

"Hi, Sunny. I got the car back, as you can see." Dell grinned from ear to ear, tossing his keys. Tracy hugged one of her pillowcases of clothes. "The old buzzard thought he had me over a barrel, but..." Dell shrugged. "You really helped us out, y'know. I won't forget it."

"That's okay, Dell. Just prove me right, okay?"

He looked up at the sun, then down at his watch. "I'll

put in a couple of hours in the yard right now, okay? Tracy, you take whichever cabin Sunny says, and get us unloaded. I'll be in after a while."

Sunny gazed at the meager holdings. It wasn't much with which to start a new life or career. She'd started with about the same, many years ago now, with a new job and determination to make something of herself shining out for all to see.

The Larsons had cheered her onward and upward. Now these kids needed that kind of encouragement.

"Never mind that, Dell. No more work tonight. You kids take cabin one. It's empty for now. Get settled. I'll cook something for supper and we can eat at my place. Then first thing tomorrow, Dell, you can begin. Okay?"

"Sure thing, Sunny. Bright and early, you betcha. I'll go into town and hire on somewhere, soon as possible. Tracy will, too…" he turned to check with Tracy, and at her nod, added, "and we'll make out."

Sunny turned to Tracy. "Nope. Tracy is now working for me, you understand? She'll clean cabins to pay the rent. You don't mind that, do you, Tracy?"

"Uh-uh. Not a bit," Tracy said, her eyes wide. "If you show me what all you want done, I'll do it. We'll make out."

"All right. Now get yourselves settled, and come on over after you do. About six, I think. We'll have something…I don't know what, because I didn't get to the grocery store today."

She'd have to remedy that tomorrow.

The two scooted the fifty yards to the first cabin, and eagerly disappeared inside. Sunny stood in the back doorway of the apartment and watched the lights go on in cabin one as they checked each room. It didn't take long. Tracy appeared at the door, Dell behind her.

"It's just perfect, Sunny. It's great!" Tracy called. She fixed her gaze earnestly on Sunny, suppressing tears. "Thank you. You're a lifesaver."

Not me, sweetie. I see the Lord's hand in this, Sunny thought to herself. "See you at six then."

Sunny went inside and right to her cupboard and refrigerator. There wasn't much there. She'd been buying for one person, and she often didn't eat much, existing mostly on frozen entrées and salads. And peanut butter sandwiches.

She made a face. She ate those too often.

There were eggs. And a little milk, thank goodness. Was it enough? Omelettes and toast came to mind. She had all the right ingredients—except butter. She'd need butter. She sucked on her fingernail.

Never mind. She'd just ask Grant.

Thirty minutes later, Grant spotted her at once while he was yet out on the lake. As he slowed his boat and carefully lined up with the dock, she caught his rope, and dropping to her knees, she began securing it to the ring provided.

"Hi, Sunny," he said and glanced up at her. "What's up?"

"Nothing much. I want to borrow some butter, if you don't mind."

"Butter?" He was astounded. He climbed out of the boat.

"Yes. I need it for dinner." She rose from her

stooped position. "I'll just follow you home for it and you won't have to come back this way. You don't mind, do you?"

"Um, no…no, of course not." He secured his boat. "I'll have to call and let…Buzz know. I—hmm…look, Sunny, with guests coming, you must be busy. Why don't I just run home and get some and come back? Butter all you need? And how much? If you're wanting it for dinner, you'll need it right away, won't you?"

"Yes…but I don't want to trouble you."

"It's no trouble. I'll do it right away. What are you making, anyway?" His curiosity ran high.

She laughed. "Omelettes and toast. I…er, have guests that I wasn't prepared for and eggs are all I have on hand." She thought a moment. "I'm not much of a cook. Perhaps it would be easier if I just took them to a restaurant in town."

"Oh, don't do that…run all the way back into town? You've been gone all day." He appeared to think faster than a runaway truck. "I have an idea. My assistant, Buzz, is making a big pot roast tonight. And vegetables. Why don't I just get it and bring it up? We can all eat together…"

"A pot roast?" The idea of a pot roast made her mouth water. She couldn't think of anything better as a welcome dinner for Dell and Tracy. "That sounds delicious."

All at once, she hesitated. It would be asking a lot for Grant to feed three unexpected guests. And how did Grant know she'd been gone all day, she thought fleetingly. He must've called, and found the office empty. But her thoughts flew back to dinner. "Are you sure you don't want us at your place? It's a lot of trouble to transport a whole dinner, don't you think?"

"Well, that would be a lot easier." His eyes were speculative. He glanced beyond her, and up the hill. "I'll just call Buzz and tell him to expect us. Let him put on a few manners."

Sunny stared at him in wonder, thinking he was a mighty easygoing kind of guy. Sometimes.

Then it dawned on her. He didn't know who her guests were. He wouldn't like it…or them.

Disappointment slid over her, but she pushed it aside. Perhaps she'd just borrow the butter after all. He'd fuss, but he'd get it for her.

"Um, Grant—"

"Hey, Grant!" A tall man, carrying fishing poles and a tackle box came down the concrete walk. Mr. Locke. From cabin four. "Long time no see, buddy! How's it going, anyway?"

"Rick, how are you?" Grant turned, and the two men shook hands. Both men grinned like Cheshire cats. "Haven't seen you since my days with, um, a couple of years, anyway. Since that fishing derby, if I'm not mistaken."

"That's right, that's right. Say, whatever happened to that girl you were engaged to? Heather?"

Grant was engaged?

"Oh, we, ah, broke up. She went on to New York, I think."

The information made Sunny first catch her breath, then let it out in a long slow sigh.

Grant paid no attention, busy exchanging information with his old friend. "I guess you haven't heard that I own a riding stable now, just down the road. Grant's Retreat."

"No! I've seen your flyer, but I didn't know it was you. Well, whatdaya know…" Rick looked impressed. "Did old Nathan sell you the land after all? He sure didn't want a noisy playmate kind of place, did he? Rabid about what was to come. Must say, the quietness of this cove is one reason we still come here."

"Yeah, he did. Sold me the piece with an option on this place when… Well, Nathan has—had his own way of doing things. He helped me get Grant's Retreat started." Grant turned to Sunny. "This is Nathan's granddaughter, Sunny. She recently inherited Sunshine Acres."

"Oh, hi ya, Sunny. Met you when I came in, didn't I?" The surprise on Rick's face didn't hide his sadness. "So old Nathan is gone, is he? I'm sorry. He was a mighty nice man, as I'm sure you know. Didn't know about his demise."

Sunny glanced at Grant while his friend was talking. He stared at the far trees, his look almost blank.

"Well," Rick continued. "I'm sorry for your loss. Guess I'm behind the times. My wife made the reservations while I was busy, and I didn't question anything."

Sunny hardly knew what to say. "Thank you, you're very kind to say that. I hope you enjoy your stay here, Mr. Locke. We plan to keep the resort understated."

"Well, nice to see you, Grant. I used to ride once in a while. Guess I can call you and we can do it any day I'm here?"

"Sure enough, Rick. Just call for reservations."

"Okay. I'll be seeing you."

Rick went on his way down the hill. Sunny and Grant watched him until he was out of earshot.

"Um, Grant?"

Grant took a step up the hill. "Yeah?"

She started after him. "I don't think I should accept your invitation for supper."

Grant turned, still walking. "Why not?"

"Well, my guests…" She hurried to keep up with him.

Grant stopped dead in his tracks. A suspicious gleam entered his gaze. He twisted his mouth, then relaxing it, said, "All right. Who are your guests?"

"Dell and Tracy."

His eyes drifted shut and he nearly groaned. "Uh-huh."

Sunny shifted her stance, opening her mouth, but before she could say anything else, he continued.

"Yeah, that would figure." His tone was one of long-suffering patience. "Dell and Tracy. Well, I suppose I can't stop you from making friends, but you're asking for trouble."

"They may be trouble, but somebody's got to help those kids, Grant." Her voice went a level higher. "They're now without a home or family or—or anything. I don't suppose you know what that's like, do you? It's like you've dropped into a big hole with nothing to grab. No way to climb up and out.…

"Unless someone helps, someone cares.… I was lucky. Blessed, actually. I found the Larsons—or rather they found me when they took me as a placement from Social Services—but not until I suffered some dreadful temporary places…lost all of my dignity and nearly my sense of who I am…almost my virginity—"

Shocked at what she'd let slip, she suddenly clamped her mouth shut. Grant couldn't know.

He stared at her while her cheeks flushed scarlet. She dropped her lashes. "I'm sorry I said that. Please forget it, will you? Please? Um…may I still borrow the butter?"

After a long moment, he shook his head. His grave stare, full of heartfelt compassion, told her he had missed none of her diatribe. Not the telling bit.

Embarrassed, she looked at her sneakers. But he spoke only about dinner.

"Nope. The invitation for dinner still stands. I don't have anything against the girl, and maybe, as you've said, Dell has grown up some."

"Her name is Tracy," she insisted.

He nodded. "Tracy. I'll remember. I'll just go and phone Buzz to expect company."

Chapter Twelve

Sunny felt a bit uncomfortable about bringing Dell and Tracy to Grant's house, but she'd dug herself in and she didn't know what else to do. She had to see it through. Yet the whole thing was rather funny, too.

Dell promised to be polite—and to watch his mouth. Even apologize, if necessary.

Tracy promised to be on her best behavior, but the child had never made an enemy of Grant. She'd never met him, only seen him about the resort.

As if Tracy could be anything else but well-behaved, Sunny thought. The poor child was afraid to give anyone a cross-eyed stare.

Grant promised to be a gracious host, he'd said with his tongue in his cheek. That made her secretly laugh. Time would tell on that one. But she was more than a little grateful for the invitation, considering the day she'd had.

She preferred not to think about her earlier outburst.

She promised herself that was the last time she'd lose her composure. She'd worked too hard for it all these years.

As for dinner, Sunny promised to enjoy the pot roast enormously. Since she'd been here at the lake, she'd rarely eaten a meal like the Larsons would've served.

They arrived promptly at six-thirty. The three-quarter-mile drive from her place narrowed over a deep hill and Sunny slowed at the approach. Then the rustic-looking ranch appeared as though it had been there for an age. They saw the peak of the barn roof first, then around the bend they spotted the corral fences and the tall reach of the barn. Across the wide yard stood a small ranch house with brown wood siding and green-trimmed windows. Two stained oak rocking chairs enhanced the wide front porch.

Sunny pulled in behind Grant's truck and parked in the curve that serviced the house. He waited on the front porch while she walked up the short stone walk.

"Welcome to Grant's Retreat," he said with a smile. He seemed to truly welcome them. He took Sunny's arm, giving her a warm look, then glanced at the two young people to include them all.

"Dinner is going to take a bit longer." He bent to pick up a bucket. Several carrots lay there. "Want to see some of my horses?"

"Yes, of course. How many do you have?" Sunny asked.

"Only twelve at the moment. But I plan to buy more next year."

As they talked they strolled down to the pasture on the other side of the barn. Five horses stood near the fence, two brown ones who looked almost exactly alike, a mottled gray gelding, a spotted mare and a brown mare with a darker mane and tail.

Sunny stared at them. They raised their heads to see if a treat was offered. Grant put his fingers in his teeth and whistled. Two of the horses ambled over to the fence.

"Do you like horses?" Grant asked Dell and Tracy.

"Like 'em well enough, I guess," said Dell. He reached a hand to pet the brown mare. "Haven't had much to do with 'em before."

"That one is Coyote. She's kind of old, but she still gets about pretty good. She doesn't seem to mind the trail at all. Why don't you pet her, Tracy?"

"Oh, um…"

"C'mon, sis. She's very gentle," said Dell.

"Here, offer her a carrot." Grant leaned over and took a carrot from the bucket, and handed it to Tracy. "Hold your palm flat, and the carrot up. Like this."

Grant illustrated the technique. The brown mare snagged the carrot in a twinkle.

Tracy laughed. "Okay, I'll try it."

Tentatively, Tracy held out her hand. Coyote moved up close to her side of the fence and slick as a whistle nuzzled the carrot from Tracy's palm. Tracy chuckled once more and patted Coyote's head. "Ooh, that tickles. This is nice, isn't it?"

A clanging began, and Grant said, "That's the dinner bell. Let's go."

They walked back to the house.

He opened the screened door into the small living room that held a dark blue sofa, two large overstuffed plaid chairs that looked worn, and an old wooden desk. A large round rug set the living room boundaries.

A huge kitchen opened from the living room, with a picnic table at one end, set for five. The stove was the surprise; it was an industrial late-model appliance. Large ovens occupied one wall, next to the island counter, and a counter down was the huge refrigerator.

Sunny glanced at Grant. It appeared he really was prepared to feed a crowd.

"How nice of you to invite us, Grant. It's nice to look forward to a decent supper." She turned and raised a brow at Dell. She was as proud as Jessica would have been when Dell didn't duck the admonishment.

Dell flushed slightly. "Um, yeah, Grant. Sure is nice. We didn't have a place to go for supper. I—I'm right…uh, sorry about, you know…being rude before. Didn't mean it, just spouting off. This sure is nice…."

Dell stumbled to a stop, glancing between Sunny and Grant while Tracy studied the floor. His eyes pleaded for his apology to be accepted.

Grant appeared a bit startled. He hadn't expected an apology from the boy and said kindly, "Let's forget all about before, Dell. We all have something we're sorry for. That's in the past."

Grant cleared his throat and glanced at Sunny. She softened her expression and nodded her approval. Grant instantly relaxed and became jovial.

"I'm glad to have you here. Actually, you're doing me a favor. I'm hoping to offer Friday- and Saturday-night suppers, so it's good to have company once in awhile so we don't become set in our ways."

"It sure beats mac and cheese," murmured Tracy, low enough for only Sunny to hear it.

Sunny placed a hand on Tracy's shoulder to reassure her.

"Let me introduce my assistant. This is Buzz."

An indeterminate age, with a short white beard and thick well-brushed hair, Buzz wore jeans and blue T-shirt with the logo Born to Love…Food, Women and Song on the front.

It made her smile.

"'Lo." Buzz uttered a scant greeting. Dell and Tracy both nodded.

"Hi, Buzz," said Sunny. "I've heard about your wonderful biscuits."

"Uh-huh…yeah," said Buzz. "Well, sit yourselves down while I dish up supper. No use it gettin' cold."

"Why don't you sit there," Grant directed Tracy and Dell. Tracy slid onto the bench against the wall. "I'll sit on the outside so I can catch the phone."

Was he expecting a call? Of course, businesses often had them at any time of the day or night.

Buzz busily went from stove to table and back to the counter as Sunny scooted into her place. She folded her hands in her lap. Tracy took her cue from Sunny and Dell followed suit.

As Grant took his seat, Buzz brought the basket with the biscuits and sat down. He reached immediately and had a hand on one, before Grant stopped him.

"Just a minute, Buzz. Sunny…that is, we like to offer grace before we eat."

All eyes turned her way. Sunny felt a flush start up

her cheeks; she felt like an untried lamb leading an un-
believing group, but she nodded and bowed her head.

"Father…we thank You for our day…" she heard
Tracy let out a long sigh, resting on it "…and this food.
We thank You for Buzz, who prepared it, and for Grant
for inviting us. In the name of the one who gives us
life…Amen."

"Now let's eat," Buzz announced.

The shadowy figure waited until almost dark, when
there was no one around. He slipped through the gloom
until he was against the front door. He'd have to hurry
now—he had to get in and get out before the girl came
home. Grant was pretty sneaky to get her down at his
place for an evening meal. Too bad he'd included that
Dell Jackson, too, but that couldn't be helped. Better
them hanging out there than here.

He edged the key in the lock as far as it would go. It
wouldn't slip into its hole all the way. He jiggled it, but
it wouldn't budge. What was wrong with it?

Glancing about him to assure himself that no one was
around to see him, he tried the key again. He sank to his
haunches and looked at the old key.

It did no good; the key wasn't working.

Dad blast it, what had the girl done to it?

Again, he carefully gazed about him. There were a
couple of guests down at the docks. He could hear them
talking. But all the others seemed content in their cabins.

He'd have to take a chance.

With swift steps, he made his way around to the
deck, and climbed the steps two at a time. He knew he

could jimmy the back door. The only problem was, it
was in view of the other cabins. If someone saw him....

He'd be inside in one short minute.

True enough, he had no trouble with the back door.
He slipped through and closed it quietly. Then he made
certain the drapes were drawn. He turned to view the
room. The lamp on the table had been left on, and he
swiftly turned it out. He didn't need a lamp to see by.

For a moment, he just stood still and sniffed. Funny,
how a place could take on a different odor with someone else in residence. The place had a less stuffy smell,
and something a bit like flowers.

He knew the place like he knew his own hand. He
made his way into the office. He wanted to check the
reservations page. An old friend was due to come in a
couple of weeks, and he hoped he wouldn't miss him.
Adversely, he hoped he could avoid him. He wasn't
ready to reveal himself to his granddaughter.

He booted up the computer and searched it till he
spotted the name he wanted. Yep, the fellow was coming with his brother. Satisfied, he turned off the computer again.

What would she do with all Grant's relatives when
they came on their annual retreat? Was she used to that
many men?

He knew he shouldn't be there, yet he was curious.
How had things changed? What was different? What
was she doing with her evenings? This was the first
time he'd had the opportunity to look around, see up
close what she'd done with the place.

A few pieces of furniture stood in different spots. The

sink was clean—he'd often left dirty dishes there. And he bet there was no dust showing, either.

He entered the bedroom, careful to flash his light onto the floor. The bed now sat at an angle, the headboard against the corner. It left no more room with which to maneuver, but it looked...better, somehow. More feminine? It gave more access to the window; he liked that.

The old picture albums sat on the floor, right next to the bed. So she was interested in the old snapshots, was she? He picked one up, flashing his light onto the front. Ah, yes. This one held pictures of Shirley and Johnny and himself.

It had been a long time since he'd looked at them; he was chicken-livered, he guessed.

He flipped through a few pages, glancing at each portrait with yearning nostalgia running fiercely through his veins. He wished with all his might that he could have those days back.

He stopped at a photo of Johnny...and then of Shirley and Johnny. They looked so young and vital.

The well-loved familiar snapshots made him sad to the point of anger. Why did *his* son have to die? Why did Johnny turn out so daring and reckless, throwing his life away in that blasted car, caring little for what his mother thought? Or himself?

Why did Shirley go so young, before she'd finished with life? She'd been only fifty-three.

He snapped the album closed with stiff fingers. That was ancient history. All water under the bridge now.

Ignoring the tears that threatened to spill, he replaced the book where it had been on the floor.

He glanced at the tiny bedside table. Books were still stacked there, but on top lay a big black Bible. Several bookmarks lay tightly squeezed inside, and he wondered what gave his granddaughter pleasure, or comfort.

Without intention, he picked up the Book and opened to where one of the bookmarks lay, balancing the flashlight so he could see the Scripture. John 6:29 was underlined: "Jesus answered 'The work of God is this: to believe in the One He has sent.'"

Nathan skipped to another passage, still in John. "Do not let your hearts be troubled. Trust in God...."

He quickly turned backward, to a marker in Matthew. It was the parable of the fig tree. "If only you believe..."

Snapping the Bible closed, he set it down.

Did she really think this stuff was true? Belief! Faith! She must. It was the top book on her night-time reading.

If he could only have a tiny bit of her faith...

Idly, he picked up one of his Westerns. It was a beloved story by a dead author, well-thumbed and worn. He'd take this with him. Might as well take a couple of others from those shelves, too. She'd never miss 'em.

But she might! Suddenly, his heart was filled with pride as he realized she was reading the books he'd enjoyed all his life.

Well, what do you know? He looked at the other titles lying there. Several of his favorites.

He shook his shoulders and straightened when he heard the car on the gravel. Speeding to the door, he peeked out. They were home early!

Starting to leave, he quickly turned back to straighten the books as he had found them. Then, with catlike steps, he slipped out the back door just as Sunny unlocked the office door.

He waited a moment in the shadows, silent as a shadow. Dell Jackson and his sister were trudging across to cabin one, calling good-night as they went.

Dell and Tracy Jackson in cabin one? How was that possible? Unless Sunny allowed them to stay there. Then he noticed the front light was on—he hadn't noticed it in context with anyone but a customer being in residence.

Blast! He narrowed his eyes, speculating on what and how. He'd have to find out about this.

Double blast! If they turned they could see him there on the deck.

He held his breath, listening. A light came on inside his—Sunny's, he reminded himself—apartment, streaming out of the windows. He edged deeper into the shadow.

He barely detected Sunny as she unlocked the door to the deck. She pushed the screen wide, then stepped out. A fragrance of something sweet and spicy met his nose. His nostrils twitched.

Did she intend to remain out on the deck all night? He'd seen her sit for a few moments before retiring of a night, while he watched from the shadows of the far trees.

For the thousandth time, he wondered what she thought about. Would she make her home here in Missouri? She was from good Missouri stock—why wouldn't she?

He didn't dare move. His gaze followed the line of her profile as she looked to the sky. Her long hair, as pale as moonlight, lay unbound across her shoulders. A low hum came from her lips, something he vaguely remembered his wife occasionally singing.

~~What was the girl planning to do now?~~

He waited until she finally went inside, then let out a breath of release. He wasn't used to waiting, but he did now—another hour, until the light in her bedroom went out. Another ten minutes, then he'd leave.

He slipped away in silence, working his way to the road. Blast it, it was darker out on the road than inside his closet until the moon rose. But he couldn't wait on that.

About halfway along the road, he heard the hum of a vehicle. He dodged into the brush beside the road.

Then he saw Grant's truck creeping along the road. Looking for him, he supposed.

He stepped out of the trees and into the headlights. The truck stopped.

"Mighty nice of ya to come find me," he muttered as he climbed into the truck. His leg ached miserably.

"I was worried about you," said Grant as he turned the truck around. He maneuvered carefully on the narrow road. "You can't go on running around late at night like this. You're likely to get yourself into a heap of trouble."

"Quit grousing. I've been running these hills since you were ten years old." Nathan leaned back against his seat, favoring his bad knee.

"Yeah, but you're not as young as you used to be."

"Don't get cheeky, Grant. I know what I'm doing."

"Boy, I sure do hope so."

"Never mind that," Nathan said, narrowing his eyes

at Grant. "Tell me what you know about those Jackson kids taking root in cabin one. I saw 'em go in, so don't try to cover."

Grant drove into the ranch yard. "Would I cover for your granddaughter?"

"You might. Can't trust nobody these days. You like her all too much."

It was telling that Grant didn't deny it.

"All I know is Sunny took up with them this afternoon. She said something about their uncle being abusive…said he was an obscene man. I guess *something* happened to Dell, all right. He had a nasty bruise on his cheek the size of a fist."

"He did, huh? Well, she's heading for trouble, if you ask me." Nathan twisted his mouth.

"Yeah, you may be right. But I gotta hand it to her. Dell apologized to me about smarting off last summer. How she got him to do that, I'll never know."

"You don't say! She never—"

"She did." Grant nodded.

"Still… What's she going to do when all your folks come and she needs that cabin? They've got to be accommodated, you know. Those kids will be out then."

"I hadn't thought that far…guess she'll figure something out." But already his mind was working. His brothers could stay with him, if they wanted. That would lessen the cabin crunch. Maybe she was counting on that.

But that wouldn't do, either. Gray and Linc knew Nathan. And Nathan held the room in the barn that Grant had fixed up for him. How would Nathan hide from them?

"It'll all work out, I suspect," Grant said with a

confidence he didn't really feel, while his speculation ran high.

He thought of all the difficulty Sunny had revealed about her teen years. There had been some harsh times—harder than she'd wanted him to know. He suspected she seldom let anyone know how hard those years were. He wished he could gather her into his arms—the overwhelming need to comfort her was strong.

He felt helpless. *God, how can I help Sunny?*

Sunny settled into the bed and lay wide awake. It had been a day to think about. Something about her long troublesome day, followed by a surprisingly delightful evening, bothered her. She couldn't put her finger on it.

The whisper of the trees outside her window no longer seemed strange, nor the night sounds. She'd left her window up for the cool night air. She welcomed it now. She gave little heed to the faint footsteps in the distance.

She sat up. Footsteps? Who was out there in the dark?

She listened carefully, supposing it was a customer, but it was gone, faded into the sounds of crickets. If only…

If only she could rid herself of this odd feeling of someone padding around at night. Watching her….

Chapter Thirteen

Sunday came, and Sunny dressed in her bright pink-flowered dress. While slipping on her matching high-heeled sandals, she felt grateful that she had a definite place to go, a worship center where she was welcomed. She longed to worship God in company.

Two separate people from the congregation had called her during the week, welcoming her to their church. It pleased her and sent a warm emotion all over her. She liked feeling as though she belonged. Liked the feeling of knowing God was everywhere. Often while growing up, she'd yearned for family. She recalled her mom telling her not long before she died, that as long as Sunny was a member of God's family, she'd never really be alone.

God's family… It gave her a mountain of hope…and faith in the future.

She wondered what Grant was doing this Sunday morning. If those church people called her, surely they'd called Grant, as well, she thought. He'd said nothing about going again.

Never mind, she told herself as she brushed her hair. She'd take Tracy with her this week. Dell was looking after the office.

She picked up her Bible and walked out to the office. Outside, it was partly cloudy, but the temperatures would climb today. She opened the door wide while the air was yet cool. Dell, in his usual jeans, was already there, pulling a weed or two until she unlocked the door.

"Good morning, Dell. How are you this morning?"

"Fine. Just fine. Tracy's almost ready to go."

"Okay. Now all the cabins but three and four should check out by noon, you know. The other two will check out tomorrow morning," she instructed. "The whole Prentiss family is coming in for a week starting tonight, so you can start cleaning the empty cabins to be ready. The rest of the family will come in tomorrow."

Sucking on her bottom lip, she softened her tone. "I hate putting you out, Dell, but the reservations were made last year. Tracy can stay with me for the week, but we'll have to find somewhere else for you to stay, I guess."

His forehead puckered. "I could sleep in the office if I had a sleeping bag. Used to sleep out as a kid, when my dad had a big tent."

"Hey, that's an idea. A tent!" Sunny said as Tracy came up the walk, wearing a denim skirt and a white sleeveless blouse. "I think I saw one in the garage. We'll look for it as soon as I get home from church. Okay, see you then."

She and Tracy climbed into Ol' Winnie and left.

A couple of hours later, when Sunny came in, Val Ferris, the kids' aunt, waited in the office. It surprised her a bit; Dell had a tight, closed expression on his face while he concentrated on the computer.

Sunny carefully laid her Bible on the desk, then turned to face the woman. This wasn't good, she surmised.

Tracy immediately pulled back, biting her lips. "Hi, Aunt Val. What are you doing here?"

"What am I doing here?" Val rose from her chair, not even trying to hide her anger, and shot Sunny an infuriated stare.

Uh-oh! Nope, this wasn't good at all.

The woman was shorter than Sunny, about thirty-five and pretty, with lots of makeup. She crossed her arms over her light-green T-shirt and spoke in clipped tones. "I came to take you home, that's what I'm doing here."

Dell's jaw was tighter than a drum. If Sunny didn't do something, he'd blow.

Sunny moved behind the counter and placed a comforting hand on Dell's shoulder. "Shut that off, Dell," she whispered. Dell nodded, and began to hit buttons.

Sunny came around the counter, idly noticing a couple of messages lying there. She picked them up, pretending to read them. Beyond the door, she saw the figure of Grant, dressed in Western clothes today, amble quietly to the open door. He leaned an arm against the door frame and watched.

She wished she could tell him to go home; Dell and Tracy wouldn't appreciate the audience. But she couldn't. This was one unpredictable situation.

Tracy came slowly forward. "I'm not going with you, Aunt Val. I'm staying here with Dell."

Good for Tracy!

"Huh!" Val tapped her high-heeled sandal. "What do you think you're playing at, my girl? You're only fifteen. The courts gave you to *me* now. You have to live with *me*."

"Took you long enough to come find us," Dell muttered between his teeth, standing behind the counter. "Three days."

Val heard it, and shot Dell a furious glance. "I was busy and couldn't get out here till this morning."

What was wrong with the telephone, Sunny wondered.

"I'm not going!" insisted Tracy.

Another man, a customer, came up behind Grant, staring over Grant's shoulder. He, too, listened attentively.

Sunny didn't say a word. She let Val continue to let her steam blow. At the same time, she let her own sigh of relief remain quiet. Like Dell, she thought Val's lack of pursuit or interest telling. Anything could have happened to those kids in the three days they'd been at Sunshine Acres; what if, instead, they'd been on the streets?

Sunny was proud of Tracy. She'd been afraid that Tracy wouldn't have the courage to say what she really wanted to do. She'd been afraid the girl would buckle.

"If you don't," Val continued "I'll have the county police out here so fast it'll make your head swim. You'll go then."

Val turned to Sunny, a sneer on her face. Then she

swung about to face the door, her hand on her hip, and when she did, she caught sight of Grant. She tossed her head and turned back to Sunny. "And I'd advise you to stay out of this if you know what's good for you, you meddling…" She bit back the name-calling. "You interfere with me or my niece one more time and I'll press charges."

At that, Sunny stood straighter. She showed a fighting readiness like a storybook heroine; her voice was hard when she spoke. "Call them. Call the sheriff. And I'll tell them of the bruise your husband gave Dell. I suspect it isn't the first time, either. I want to talk to them about Clyde threatening Tracy, too. His—"

"Sunny," whispered Tracy. The child hung her head, pleading, "Sunny, don't…."

Tracy's shame and embarrassment was more than Sunny could stand. She walked over to put her arm around the girl's shoulders, and felt her trembling. She tried to absorb it, tried to infuse Tracy with her own strength.

"I fought him off, he didn't get to me," Tracy said low. "I couldn't tell Aunt Val. How—how did you know?"

"I suspected, honey," Sunny whispered into Tracy's ear. "I just…I've faced similar things."

Val listened, suspicion crumbling her face.

"You're lying!" Val shifted her gaze from Tracy to Dell and back again, trying to hide her doubts of the truth.

"No, she isn't," interrupted Dell. "Tracy doesn't lie. Clyde is nothing but a stinking ugly pig."

"Clyde wouldn't!" Val looked askance at Tracy. At Tracy's nod, some of the belligerence dropped from her voice. She said, "You mean to tell me that Clyde tried…he made a play for you?"

Tracy merely nodded once more, looking scared, fighting tears.

Emotions flickered lightning-quick over Val's face. She fought her rising anger while trying to take in what Tracy had said. She made an effort to bluff. "I'll see…"

Swallowing, Val tried again. "I'll have a little talk with Clyde. He doesn't mean anything when he's playing around, he's only funning."

Tracy merely stared at Val.

"Funning like that can be dangerous," Sunny's voice held a hard note. "Do you still want to call the county sheriff?"

"Well, I…" Val looked sideways at Grant. She hitched her purse up to her shoulder. "Um, maybe we should talk this out. If Clyde promises not to bother you anymore, Tracy, maybe we can get along."

Please, Lord. Give Tracy the backbone she needs, Sunny prayed. *Don't let her fold.*

"I'm not going home with you, Aunt Val." Though she spoke in a near-whisper, nevertheless Tracy held firm. "I—I want to stay with Dell."

"Oh, Dell!" Val threw the name down as though it were odious garbage. "What can he do for you?"

"He's my brother, Aunt Val. I want to stay with him."

"But what will people think… I mean, Social Services will ask questions…"

Tracy continued to shake her head.

"But what will you do if I leave you on your own?" Val whined. "You can't just live on the streets."

"They won't have to live on the streets," Sunny stated. "At least not for this year. They can live here until Dell is twenty-one."

Sunny had no idea when Dell's birthday was and hoped it was within a few months. "And then he can pursue legal guardianship of Tracy until Tracy is old enough to take care of herself."

Enlightenment bloomed on Dell's face. Relief was a welcome sight.

"I can do that? Really?" Dell turned to his aunt. It seemed he'd matured in one long moment. "Sure, I'll do that, Aunt Val. Tracy's almost sixteen now. We'll get along."

Val sputtered, "But—but—"

"I'd advise you either to consult with a lawyer, call the county sheriff or go home, Mrs. Ferris. Tracy is staying," Sunny said.

"All right, then." Val narrowed her eyes, while pushing her purse up her arm. "But you haven't heard the last of this, Miss High-and-Mighty. The law's on my side in this matter."

Val marched toward the door, tossed a sour look at Grant, then went out to her car. She climbed in, and drove away in a cloud of dust.

They all blew out a collective breath.

"Whew!" said Grant. He looked admiring and relieved all at the same time. The guy behind him made an excuse and went away. "That was some piece of family drama."

"Yeah." Dell grinned with triumph.

Tracy was shaking uncontrollably, and Sunny put an

arm around her again. "It takes a long time to get something to court these days, Tracy. You're safe for a long while."

Sunny didn't know how Missouri courts worked, but she was betting that it would take a while.

"Come on, I'll make you a cup of tea. You need to settle down and think what this will mean to you and Dell. Dell will be working full-time somewhere by the time it comes to court, and he can ask for guardianship. You're getting along just fine right now, aren't you? Why, I'll bet it'll be Christmas before anything can be done through the courts."

"Sure thing, Tracy," said Dell, his eyes sparkling. "I'll go into town first thing tomorrow morning and look for work. Someone will be hiring."

Sunny turned to Grant. She could hardly keep her own mouth from curving into a smile. "Hi, Grant. What can I do for you today?"

"Nothing, I guess." He laughed. "Looks like you're taking care of things just fine."

Shaking his head, he continued, "I just wanted to explain that I had riders this morning, and that was why I couldn't go to church with you. Wanted to go, but I'd booked these people a couple of weeks ago. I won't book for Sunday mornings again."

Oddly, the promise made her feel lighter. He hadn't owed her any explanation.

"I'll go with you next week," he finished.

"Think I'll go search the garage for that tent, if you don't mind, Sunny," Dell said amiably. "Got a spot down by the edge of the lake all picked out."

"You go right ahead, Dell." Sunny handed Dell the garage keys. "Want to go with him, Tracy?"

It would give the two a few moments of privacy. Tracy jumped at the offer. "Yeah, you bet, Sunny. We won't be that long."

"Think those two will really be okay?" Grant asked, watching the two walk toward the garage.

"If I don't miss my guess, they will be." Sunny sighed. "How about that tea? Only over a long tall glass of ice, if you don't mind."

"Sounds just right. Then I've got to scoot. Have more riders this afternoon."

The rest of the day seemed rather anticlimactic, but Sunny went about her office duties with a light spirit. Dell and Tracy cleaned the cabins, and by four she was checking in the men of the Prentiss family tree.

Two minutes after four the first car pulled up; it was a late-model red SUV piled to the ceiling with fishing poles, equipment and groceries, pulling a fancy motor boat. Three people tumbled out of the car, enthusiasm high, a dark-headed man and two kids about twelve and ten.

"Grant, ol' buddy, how are you?" said the man, clasping Grant's shoulder and reaching for his hand.

Grant had shown up about ten minutes previously.

"I'm fine, Wally, just fine," Grant said, returning the greeting, shaking hands warmly. "It's good to see you. Did you drive all the way from Iowa today? How's your wife?"

Wally grinned widely. He had strong features that were reflected in the older boy's face. "Eileen's fine. Went to visit her mother."

"Your boys are sure growing."

"Yep, they are." Wally removed his yellow baseball cap to wipe his forehead. "Come here, Kyle, Darren, you remember my cousin, Grant, don't you? He's down here permanently now. Got a riding stable hereabouts, I understand."

"Uh-huh. Just down the road. You boys didn't come down last year, so you didn't see it. But I'll take you all on a long morning ride along about Tuesday or Wednesday."

The boys whooped. "Really?" Darren asked.

"Come on, I'll help you unload, soon as you check in with Sunny."

The two men talked as they went into the office. Sunny was introduced, and then Dell and Tracy. Sunny checked them in, all the while listening to family gossip—news of the widely spread family.

She smiled when the check-in was complete. "Cabin two, Mr. Taylor. I hope you'll be comfortable."

"Thanks," Wally said. "I'm going to do nothing but loaf around and fish."

Grant had no more finished carrying in a couple of bags for Wally than a second vehicle parked alongside the first.

"Dad!" he shouted as he hurried forward.

Sunny peeked from the office window. She'd often observed families in the doctor's office, and was curious about Grant's relationship with his father. Did they get along? Respect each other?

"Grant…good to see you, son." The two smiling men clasped each other in an enormous bear hug. "Brought you some of Mom's brownies. Know you've missed 'em. How's things going down at the stable since last Thursday?"

Thursday? Grant must've talked to them on the phone. She moved to the open door, unashamedly listening.

Grant's dad was a handsome man with salt-and-pepper hair, Sunny soon learned he had as strong a personality as his offspring. In his fifties, his name was Thomas Prentiss.

Grant's brother Linc climbed from the car more slowly. Skinny and lanky, the youth had a heavy history book in his hand, and left his finger in to mark the spot where he was reading.

"Gray's coming later tonight, if he can get away. He's working very hard on a case." Thomas explained, his fingers on his hips. "The boy could really use the vacation. He puts in too many hours."

"Sure, sure. That's Gray for you. Well, a vacation is what we plan on giving you, Dad." He turned to his brother. "Hiya, Linc. How's the studying going?"

"Good." Linc peered through thick glasses. "I'm going be caught up by the time school starts."

What had happened that Linc was behind? Had the boy been ill? Sunny wondered.

"That's just great, Linc. Knew you could do it." Grant said.

Grant turned to Sunny. "This is Sunny Merrill. I told you about her."

"Yes, you did." Thomas came forward and held out his hand, studying her as he did. "I'm glad to meet a grandchild of Nathan's. He must have been very proud to have found you, my dear."

"I—um, thank you. I hope he was. But I never met Nathan. He was gone by the time I even knew he existed."

"Oh?" Thomas swiftly glanced at Grant. But by the time Sunny's glance shifted to Grant, he'd appeared to forget his curiosity. "Oh, well, that's too bad. Well, well."

Grant spoke. "Get checked in, Dad, then we can visit."

"Sure thing, Grant. Say, how's the fishing? Catch anything lately?"

"Yeah, the crappie have been biting pretty good lately."

The evening progressed the same way; Grant was there to welcome each one of his cousins and uncles.

Along about bedtime, it struck Sunny that her intense curiosity about Grant's family went beyond the norm. As she made up Tracy's bed on the sofa, she wondered why that was.

Grant's family was large, and they seemed to genuinely care about each other. Only the Larsons had shown that kind of devotion, in her experience. In her work as a charge nurse, she had kept her barriers up; she hadn't met any close families, and if she had, it was only for business.

She hadn't allowed anyone in, she mused. Not for a long time. She and her mother had been close, but it was no use to yearn for what she didn't have.

Still, she thought of Grant…. He was close to his family.

Chapter Fourteen

The week had been so full that Sunny fell into bed that Sunday night with thankfulness. Some of the Prentiss family were checked in. They were a happy, boisterous lot, inclined to ask for little, but they took over the resort in a benign sort of way. The kids ran loose, but were mainly well-behaved. They just asked a million questions, squabbling amiably.

Sunny laughingly accommodated them as she could.

That night she settled Tracy on her sofa, hoping Dell was comfortable with the old ragged tent they'd found. They'd found a couple of sleeping bags, too. Sunny had aired them all day over the rail of her deck. Dell seemed content, treating the situation as an adventure, and set the tent up on the sand at the edge of the lake. The boys, Kyle and his brother Darren helped him, with Dell teasing all the way, and the whole thing was accomplished with great lightness.

She hoped it didn't rain, though. Dell could get wet.

Sunny heard the boats go out early the next morning. It was foggy, but that didn't slow them down.

"Brr...it's downright chilly sleeping at the lake's edge." Dell remarked, rubbing his hands together when he showed up at the office early for breakfast. "But I don't mind. I'll just have to keep the kids out of my tent."

Tracy set out cereal and whole-wheat toast while Sunny got dressed, and first Dell, then Tracy took their showers while she worked in the office.

The daily pattern was set.

She had no earthly idea Grant would be spending every spare moment at her place, but he was there that afternoon, while the rest of the group checked in, greeting each other with happy smiles, slaps on the back and challenges—who would catch the biggest fish, who would win at cards, and when they learned that Grant had built a horseshoe-pitching court, who would win that.

Sunny laughed all over again, hearing it.

Then the early fishermen from the group returned, lugging strings of fish. They ate them for lunch, cooked over the outdoor grill. Then they napped or sat about with the kids, telling stories or playing games. The kids batted about the birdie to the badminton, but the net sagged. That night some of them went out to fish again.

Tuesday was a repeat of Monday. In the following days, Grant was there as often as not, when he had time off from the stables. Sunny watched him from afar whenever he was there, laughing a lot with his brothers, playing jokes with his uncles or telling stories, playing tag with the boys, running races with the older ones or taking any of them out in his boat.

True to his word, he'd made a horseshoe court down beyond his barn. The guys ambled down there after supper one night to play, view the ranch and ride. Sunny spent the quiet evening sitting at the dock, watching the sunset. She enjoyed the solitude, something she'd only recently come to love.

But when he had customers, Grant tended to business and didn't come around or invite any of his family along.

The time grew flat without Grant around…

But Sunny had other things to think about. Dell and Tracy, for instance.

First thing Monday morning, after Dell used her bathroom to clean up and put on his best jeans, he'd gone into town to look for work. He came home about three in the afternoon, and though tired, he cleaned the docks. He said nothing about where he'd gone or the applications he'd made.

Sunny bit her tongue, worrying about Dell. She refused to ask, thinking it none of her business. Tracy would know, and that was all that was necessary.

Tracy, though… Tracy proved to be a surprise. She jumped out of bed each morning, folded up her quilt and sheets, helped with breakfast and cleanup and was ready to tackle anything Sunny set her to doing. Sunny noticed Tracy especially liked the outdoors, sometimes playing with the little guys if they were about, but she proved to be a whiz at the computer.

Sunny even had time to look at the appliance catalog, thinking to install small apartment-size washers and dryers in each cabin. The clothesline between two of the cabins held sloppy wet towels and swimsuits most days, but that clothesline wouldn't entice customers to stay a little longer. Most resorts had washers and dryers these days.

I'm thinking of how to improve these cabins every day, Sunny thought. *They will sell better with those appliances installed.*

Hmm…they'll sell much faster painted and with a few repairs, too. I'll put Dell on it soon after Labor Day.

She wouldn't think about that now, Sunny decided. It would be months until she had the freedom to sell this place. Way after the holidays. She could stand to wait until the slower winter season to make the repairs.

"So why don't you go on into town? Take care of getting your washer and dryer?" Grant asked on Tuesday morning as he hung around waiting for his dad to return from his morning fishing.

Sunny had fussed too much in his hearing, she decided.

"Well, with Dell gone," she tossed a pencil from hand to hand. "I need to stay around in case someone needs something."

"Why?" Grant's eyes looked bluer, against the blue ball cap he wore. He pushed it to the back of his head. "All the guys are happy. They're grown-ups. You could be gone all day and they wouldn't notice."

"But—"

"No buts. You're covered. Tracy can take care of the phone."

Sunny really needed to replace the old appliances out in the garage, and soon. Even with hiring a laundry service for the bed linen, she was tired of running into town each time she wanted to wash her own clothes.

"All right?" Sunny asked, tossing the pencil to the desk and gazing at Tracy with a question in her eyes.

"Yeah, Sunny." Tracy's eyes shone with excitement over being put in charge. She swung around in the swivel chair. "I can take care of the office for a little while. Go on."

"Might as well," Sunny murmured. She hurried into her apartment to change clothes.

"Dad's coming," she heard Grant say. Listening as she picked up her keys and purse, she heard the faint hum of a boat. She wondered how Grant knew it was his father's boat instead of any of a dozen out on the lake.

As she started the truck, she saw Grant disappearing over the hill toward the docks in her rearview mirror.

But his head was turned her way, watching her leave.

Lifting a hand, she waved. Then she smoothed back her hair. She doubted she'd have left without his encouragement. Now…to the appliance store in town. It was the only one in town. She laughed at that. Who would've guessed she could get along without the huge stores of a big city?

But it wouldn't take long; she knew exactly the heavy-duty models she wanted. It might take a chunk of her savings, but she thought it a good investment for the future.

"I'll have delivery out your way by Thursday, Miss Merrill," promised the young sales lady after thirty minutes. "And they'll be hooked and you can use them by Thursday evening."

"Just dandy," said Sunny. She felt positively reckless. "Now could you direct me to the best store to buy bed linens?"

She was directed to another town, about seventeen miles away, to the discount store everyone used.

Ah, well. She might as well go. She could use the replacement sheets no matter what. What would they cost?

She drove the seventeen miles, gazing at the scenery all the way. She hadn't had time to do much exploring since she'd been in residence. Every once in a while she caught glimpses of the vast expanse of the lake and marveled at its beauty and size. It stretched farther than she could see. No apartment buildings, no closely built houses, no busy streets. But a few high-rise condos lay down that road, she knew, and there were more in the next cove. As she got closer to town, crowded recreation centers, restaurants and novelty attractions lined the streets.

Whew! No wonder her grandfather had protected the small cove where Sunshine Acres was located. It was a treasure.

She recognized the grocery store where Clyde had hidden Dell's car. That reminded her of half a dozen things she should get there. She'd make a quick stop before going home.

It was a far different lifestyle than any she'd known in the past. There wasn't a straight road here. Had Grant found it hard to adjust after being raised in a big city? What did he do in the wintertime? Did he close his retreat altogether?

She reached the store that had been recommended, and spent time looking at the sheets. She finally settled for four sets of plain white. She could throw away those torn ones she'd found a couple of days ago. These would do until she could afford to replace the beds. But she dreamed of pastel colors on fresh mattresses that would brighten the bedrooms.

She shook her head. Taking care of business was the best thing to occupy her thoughts, instead of dwelling on the troubles of Dell and Tracy and…Grant! The guy was having a whale of a good time with the men of his family here.

But he was taking way more of her thoughts than was good for her.

The sun lay low in the western sky as Sunny lingered by the lake. The boys were there swimming. She strolled the premises hearing the boys shout and laugh while playing in the roped-off area designated for swimming. It made her smile to see them and she waved. One of the fathers watched over them, Connor, she thought.

She heard a boat approaching. Grant and his dad. The boat slowed and gently bumped into its mooring. Grant hopped out and secured it.

Sunny strolled down.

"Hi, Sunny. Can you use some fish?" Thomas Prentiss held up a string of good-looking crappie and bass.

"Thanks, but no thanks. We've had supper. Besides, the only kind of fish I know how to cook comes from a grocery-store freezer."

"Oh, too bad. Fresh fish are the best tasting. You ought to get Grant to show you how to fillet them, then grill them. You can't beat that for supper."

"I will." She couldn't help glancing at Grant. What would he have to say about his father offering his cooking services?

Grant grinned at her and raised an eyebrow. "Sure, Sunny. Let me show you what to do…er, how to cook fish some time."

She snorted. Grant showing her what to do? *Give me a break. What would you teach me?*

Nonetheless, her heart began to pound at the thought of him teaching her anything. "You?"

Grant raised his eyebrow once more, teasing, "Think I can't?"

"Hi, Uncle Thomas," yelled one of the swimmers just then.

"Hi, guys," called Thomas. "Having fun?"

"Yeah," they called in unison.

"You better believe it," Connor raised his voice to add. "They'll be so waterlogged by the time we start for home I'll have to wring them out with a rolling pin."

Then Thomas said more conversationally, "The boys always have a lot of fun in the water. They'd rather swim that eat."

"Yes, they seem to," remarked Sunny, watching them.

"They'd be in the lake all day if we let 'em. But as long as an adult is with them," observed Thomas "and they don't get too much sun, it's all right."

"Hmm, maybe Tracy would like to swim sometime. She could watch over the boys a couple of afternoons for you."

Sunny had no idea what Tracy's swimming credentials were like, but she knew the girl could swim. She'd check as soon as she could. The girl needed the outdoor activity as much as anyone.

She recalled when her mother taught her to swim.

They'd had such a good time, laughing joyously and playing in a friend's pool that summer when she was…nine, was it? Or ten? It was a rarity for them to be invited to a private pool. It was the last time her mother had laughed so freely. Soon after, her mother became sick and the following year, she died.

That was the last time Sunny'd shared laughter with her mom. She hadn't connected it till now…the swimming and the laughter.

"Hey, that would be super," said Grant cheerfully. "Give the boys a break by swimming with a pretty girl, and the bigger guys can get in a little chess."

Sunny forced a chuckle, but it hurt her throat. She swallowed, hoping to get rid of the lump there, and turned to watch the kids a minute longer.

"Well, I'll take these up," said Thomas, and started up the hill. "Quicker they're on ice the better."

"I'll be along in a little while, Dad."

Sunny abruptly turned and started up away from the two men—from the swimmers and laughter. The old hurt reared with sudden ferocity, of being left without a mom, of being an orphan, of having no one who cared. She impulsively headed toward the trees.

"Hey, Sunny!"

She continued walking, her strides long and hurried. Out of habit, she hid her tears.

"Sunny?"

She suddenly felt his hand catch her arm; she stopped, poised at the edge of her usually cool nerves, but kept her head turned away from him. She wiped her eyes with the heel of her hand.

"Uh-oh. You're crying."

"No, I'm not."

Yet her voice wobbled.

"Well, it looks like it to me." He bent his head to view her face. "Why? Why are you crying?"

"It's nothing. Really."

"It's *something*." He insisted.

"It's only your family…no, I don't mean that… It— it's the swimming… I just remembered my mother teaching me to swim. It was the last good time we had. The last time I heard her laugh."

"Ah, Sunny. I'm sorry, sweetheart." He leaned in to kiss her gently on the forehead, placing his palm against her cheek. "I'm sorry your memories aren't better."

"No, no. They're good." She gazed up at him, stumbling with what truth to tell him. "My mother was a fine person. Just too young to…well, too young. She always thought my paternal grandparents didn't want anything to do with us, you see. So she taught me about God, about His Fatherhood, and being a part of His family. I can name a half dozen churches we attended before she died." Her bottom lip began to tremble. "It was enough. Only…afterward…afterward was hard."

His gaze softened as she spoke, as if he should say something, but didn't know what. Then he lowered his head to place his mouth on hers.

It felt as soft and gentle as the lake breeze. She'd been a long time without comfort…

But the comfort vanished as longing swooshed into flame.

She pushed to her tiptoes to reach his mouth better.

He smelled of fresh air and sunshine, and tasted faintly of coffee. Realization came drifting through her hazy thoughts—she'd wanted to feel his kiss since…since she'd met him?

His arms tightened, making her feel cared for…very cherished. It filled her, slowly spreading from her middle until she felt it to her fingertips.

Then the kiss suddenly exploded like a Fourth of July firecracker.

He slowly withdrew, gazing at her with warm intensity. She stared back, her mind whirling, the impression of his lips lingering. Her breath came in shallow little gasps.

"Whoa!" he said softly. He blinked, seemingly in disbelief.

"Yeees…" she murmured.

She turned and stumbled away.

Chapter Fifteen

Gray Prentiss didn't arrive until Tuesday afternoon. He looked a lot like Grant, but weary, with stronger, more clear-cut features. He had the same wide smile, showing strong white teeth, as his father and Grant…

But Grant's smile was cuter.

Gray didn't come out of his cabin until late the next day, and he lounged on the deck in only a pair of cut-off jeans.

Nice legs, Sunny thought. But then Grant had nice legs, too—strong and shapely. Grant had appeal…

Now why was she doing that again? Thinking of Grant? She shoved the thoughts behind her with a vengeance; just because Grant's smile was more attractive than…and his eyes held a gleam sometimes…

That was all she needed, she scolded herself. After only one kiss, she had feelings she didn't plan to pursue. The trouble was, she didn't know exactly what to do with it. It was no use becoming accustomed to Grant being around all the time, when in less than a year…

Only a year? Why couldn't she…no, it was better not even to think it. She'd learned never to count on anything.

Sunny didn't like letting Grant have too much of her, know her too well, it wasn't…wise. Not wise for her, anyway. And she'd been letting him in since—since day one, when she'd first met him. She didn't want to know too much of Grant, either. People seemed to die, or go away somehow when Sunny loved them.

Well, she wouldn't love Grant. She only liked him a lot. There wasn't anything wrong with that.

The sun was hot this morning. She went to close the office blinds and turn on the overhead fan.

She turned to study her registration list for next week. How many were there? Enough for the moment. She'd been at Sunshine Acres long enough to know that some customers came in at the last moment.

When her year was up, and she sold the resort, what then?

She'd go back to Minneapolis. Perhaps.

That gave her pause. She'd never given thought of going anywhere else to live. But she had only the Larsons as a tie. They were important to her.

Dell and Tracy would have to find somewhere else to live—but they would be one year older and more likely to be able to cope with life on their own.

Grant would remain…his riding stable would continue.

She'd have to get another job if she went back to Minneapolis. Her old position was filled by now.

But with both Dell and Tracy at the resort to look after the daily things, why couldn't she get a job in town? That would be the thing.

She hadn't taken the time to look at the local hospital yet, she reminded herself. But hospitals could always use nurses. If she took a part-time position, she could pay for those appliances in a jiffy on monthly installments. After all, she was paying no rent here.

Why not? After the Prentiss clan left, she'd do that.

True to his word, Grant took some of the crowd riding on Tuesday morning, and a second group on Wednesday morning. Some of the men discovered the horseshoe court down by Grant's barn, declaring in Sunny's hearing how great the game was.

Gray was too tired to go horseback riding. But on Friday, Grant urged his brother to come see his resort, and Gray eagerly consented.

Grant asked Sunny to ride at the same time.

"Do you have room for Tracy to go, too?" Sunny asked tentatively.

Grant's smile was lopsided with acceptance. "Sure, why not. Even Dell, if he wants to. But you'll have to follow orders, since I've five riders who are paying customers. With Gray, Tracy, and you, that'll make eight. We can accommodate as many as ten if need be."

Sunny had only ridden twice in her life, Tracy never. It took some coaxing.

"Come on, Tracy. It'll be fun." Sunny tipped her head. Sunny didn't want to be the only one to go along with the two Prentiss men.

"For who?" Tracy was dubious.

"For you and me," promised Sunny. "Come on, honey, you've been to the ranch and seen the horses. And you've been holed up here at Sunshine Acres for a few days now. You need to get out and have some fun. Those horses are all broke to ride."

"She doesn't have to come if she doesn't want to," said Grant, leaning against the counter. "But it would be very cool if you came, Tracy. Another accomplishment to add to your résumé. You can even tell your friends about the ride. Think of it as advertising for me." He finished with a grin.

"Okay, but you have to give me the gentlest horse," Tracy said, tossing a doubtful look at him. "That's Coyote, isn't it?"

"Yep. You learned something the other night, didn't you?"

Chuckling, Sunny told Grant, "I hope you know you're taking a bunch of amateurs out."

"Oh, I know, all right," Grant said with amusement in his eyes. "Happens all the time. Most of my horses are gentle for that reason. But it'll be a good ride, I guarantee you. I've got customers to satisfy."

"That's good, I suppose." Underneath it all, she felt more than a little excitement. It must be an accumulation of all that was going on in her life, she decided.

"We're going late in the afternoon," Grant continued. "The customers wanted to get a ride in about four, just before suppertime. It'll be a short ride. We'll only be out an hour or so."

"All right then," said Sunny. "Sounds perfect. I suppose Dell will be home by then. He's sure putting in his applications."

Dell not only came home by two o'clock, he came home with a job.

"I knew you could do it!" Tracy was jubilant.

So was Sunny. She chuckled. "I did, too. There's no moss on you, my friend."

"I start tonight," Dell said with a bit of pride. "I'll have to leave Tracy at night though," he said worriedly. "I'll be stocking shelves at the grocery store. It'll bring in a steady income, but... Could you keep an eye on Tracy for me, Sunny?"

"I'm old enough to keep an eye on myself!" Tracy protested.

"Sure," Sunny said. "But I think you'll need to sack out for a time this afternoon, don't you?" Sunny pointed through to the apartment. "You can take the sofa, in there."

"Are you sure?" An uncertain, incredulous light entered Dell's eyes. "Don't know what we did to deserve all the kindness, Sunny. But I—I'm grateful."

The parable of the little children coming to Jesus loomed up in her mind, suddenly large and unmistakable. Dell and Tracy were no longer children, yet in her mind they were. By taking them in, she was following Jesus' teachings.

"Yeah, I know." Sunny said softly, inwardly groaning for the dozenth time. How did she get herself into these things?

But she knew... She really knew.

Sunny and Tracy left the resort soon afterward, leaving Dell asleep, tiptoeing out so they wouldn't wake him. Sunny set the alarm clock and placed it on the table near his head. In the normal scheme of things, he'd be gone by the time they returned.

Excitement bubbled along her veins at the prospect of sampling Grant's business firsthand. She and Tracy wore jeans and long-sleeved shirts. Neither had hats against the late-afternoon sun, but Sunny didn't think that necessary; as she understood it, they'd be in the woods a good deal of the time. They were ready to ride.

When they reached Grant's Retreat, Sunny and Tracy stood back and watched the scene. Gray was already there, leaning against the corral. The horses waited, saddled and ready. The customers arrived within minutes of the stated time, talking together excitedly.

Grant was purely professional as he checked each horse, each saddle, then assigned riders. He moved with quick assurance, never missing a step. Buzz helped the customers into the saddle, checked the length of stirrups, and then lined up the horses one by one.

Grant turned his attention to Tracy and her. Oh, my! Sunny felt her heart pick up its beat. He looked like a real cowboy: boots, hat and cool demeanor.

She noticed Gray, dressed in jeans and long-sleeved checked shirt, quietly observing the scene as each member of their party mounted. Then he came forward with slow, lanky strides and mounted Pepper, a horse speckled around the flanks that Grant had assigned him.

"Thanks, Grant," Gray said graciously. But he wasn't nearly as compelling as Grant.

"Tracy, here you are," Grant called the girl over to the old brown mare with the black mane. "Coyote, per your request."

Tracy tentatively walked forward, and Grant helped her up into the saddle. Buzz adjusted her stirrups.

"Now, Sunny," Grant said, indicating the horse she would ride. His mouth curved slightly, as though teasing her, warm and personal. "Her name is Ginger," he said, slapping the horse's neck. "And you'll bring up the rear, if you don't mind, so you can keep an eye on Tracy. I want to watch that couple up front. If I'm not mistaken, they're not beyond mischief."

"Sure, Grant." She carefully mounted, and the ginger-colored horse sidestepped a bit.

"Whoa, there, Ginger." His grin came and went in a flash. "Can't have any of that playfulness."

Grant then mounted a dappled gray, a bright-eyed gelding, and took the lead. Sunny reined her horse back to follow Gray and Tracy.

They entered the forest at the bottom of the pasture, then began to climb. The trail led around a hill, ever climbing. They passed hickory, maple, oak and walnut trees. Everything was green, and smelled of moist earth from the slight rain they'd received the night before. The ground was mostly covered in old leaves and green brush, with the occasional fallen tree.

An oak leaf drifted down; she watched it land in front of her. She gazed up. It wasn't autumn yet, but they were in the last month of summer. She could see the tops of the trees, some forty feet high.

Sunny looked to see if Tracy were enjoying the ride. The dreamy expression answered the question, but she was holding on for dear life.

They came to a stop at the top of the hill, resting for five minutes, and then started down. They came upon a wide gash in the earth, and Sunny felt Ginger plunge down the side of it at a good clip and then bounce back up again. Coming down was a different experience than going up, Sunny mused.

They came out of the woods into the same small meadow, sunny and peaceful, surprising Sunny with its beauty. The back of the barn showed in the distance. Another ten minutes, and they'd be in the home corral.

Buzz was on hand to help the riders dismount. They were laughing and calling back and forth. "Thanks a lot, Mr. Prentiss," the young woman called. "We had a good time."

"Glad you liked the ride…and come again."

"Oh, we'll come again when next we come to the lake," the dark-eyed woman promised. "And we'll tell our friends about you. Bye now."

The riding company, one woman and four men got in their cars and left while Sunny eased off Ginger, patting her after she dismounted.

Behind her, Tracy slid off Coyote. "That was cool. Wait till I tell my friends at school."

All her apprehensions gone, Tracy talked a blue streak. She chattered as Buzz took the reins.

"Good ride, Grant. I'd like to do the longer trail sometime," said Gray. He dismounted and approached his brother. "Your idea for developing this into a full working ranch is a good one. Let me know if I can help out."

"Thanks, Gray. I appreciate that," Grant said, starting to unsaddle the horses. Standing next to him, Gray unsaddled his own mount.

Grant continued. "But that remains to be seen. I want to expand, but…" He glanced Sunny's way, then lowered his tone. "I hope to develop more of the trail by the end of two more years. Add some cattle as a sideline, too. I should have enough trade by then to warrant longer rides."

Grant still wanted the land she held, Sunny thought. He needed it; it would make a good package.

She sighed deeply. Nothing had really changed, and his kiss hadn't meant nearly as much to him as it had meant to her.

Somewhere inside her, just a little something twisted. Did Grant like her for herself, or did he like her for what she could do for him? Such as sell him the land....

Saturday dawned bright and hot, the last day for the Prentiss clan. Already some of the men showed an anxiety to get back to civilization...and their wives and daughters, mothers and girlfriends. The kids didn't, but then kids never did, Sunny thought with amusement.

Along about three o'clock, Grant drove in and came into the office. He eyed the stacked linen on the desk chair. A basket holding cleaning products, scrub brushes and rags were on the floor.

"Sorta eager for the family to be gone, eh?" he remarked.

"Not at all, Grant." She smiled at him, hoping he knew she'd welcome his family any time. "They've been great guests and I hate to lose them. But since some of them will leave at first light, we want to be ready. It's the last week before school starts for some families. For Tracy, too."

"Um, sorry." Grant appeared somewhat shamefaced.

"That sounded kind of…oh, you know. I didn't mean it to be grumpy."

Sunny sighed and rose from her chair to hang over the counter, facing him. She played with a string she'd found on the floor. "I suppose you hate the idea of your relatives leaving. It's been fun. I'm sure you like having them all down and hanging about each day."

"Yeah. Except for Mom. I miss her and my sis, Ginny. But I'll take a run up to Kansas City soon and see them."

"What did you come by for, anyway?"

"Oh, um, well, um," he said as he leaned his arms on the counter, running his finger against the edge of it. "I just…I sorta wanted to suggest that you and Tracy might like to go to a movie this evening. Have dinner out, and shop or something."

"I don't know, Grant. I don't think we should."

Sunny turned to glance through the door to the apartment. Out of sight, Tracy sat out on the deck, reading.

"Well, you really should go, Sunny. It's…you haven't been out in a while."

Only inches away, Sunny's fingers curled the string. "Only down to your stable."

Shifting his feet, he grinned as he leaned closer. "Well, that doesn't count. You should really get out."

"Well, there's church tomorrow."

"That doesn't count, either."

"Okay, then. Why? What's going on?"

Grant cleared his throat, reaching for her fingers. "Okay, guess I'll have to tell you straight out."

"That might be nice," she said as his fingers played with hers. "The truth always works."

"Well, it's this way. The Prentiss men always celebrate their last night with a swimming party."

"Oh, that's no problem." She withdrew her hand.

"It is if you hang around." He turned his hands to lay them flat on the counter.

"Why? What have I got to do with a swimming party?"

"Nothing. Er, you're a woman. Tracy is, too."

"Oh, only men allowed, hmm?" She folded her arms.

"Yes, that's it. But I think it might be better if you're off the premises altogether."

"But why?" She raised a brow.

He looked very serious. He drew a deep breath and took the plunge. "Okay, okay. They like to swim in the raw."

She stood with her mouth open for five full seconds before bursting into laughter. A faint flush stole up Grant's cheeks.

"Glad you think it's funny," he muttered.

"Is that all?" She dropped her hands. "You think that I'll peek? Or Tracy will? Why, that's the dumbest thing I've ever heard. Besides, as a nurse, I've seen my share of bodies. I'm not one iota curious."

"But the men will be happier if you're not here."

"Oh, I see." She twisted her mouth, trying not to laugh further. "Well, then, I guess Tracy and I will find some entertainment in town."

"That's what I hoped you'd say." A huge sigh escaped from him. Now that Grant was off the hook, he relaxed. "You ought to try it sometime."

"What, swimming in the nude?"

"Nah, I—I didn't mean that." He recovered quickly. "I meant take a swim at dusk, while the sun is sinking. You haven't been swimming yet, have you?"

"No, I haven't. I've been too busy, and it seemed kind of intrusive to swim with the guests."

"Well, yeah, I can see it that way myself. But you have the perfect spot, rather secluded and not in the main part of the lake. In August when the water is warm, the nights can be soft. Swimming just before bedtime… It's great, better than a sauna! You even sleep better."

"I'll have to try it sometime."

"Not alone, though. You shouldn't ever swim alone."

"No, I wouldn't. I'll be sensible."

"Okay, then. Can I tell the fellas, hmm…about what time?"

"The time Tracy and I will leave?"

"Yes."

"Oh, I think soon after four. Tracy and I can find something to do for those hours between four and supper, and then a movie. The movie will be out, oh, say nine-thirty or so, then if we get an ice cream, we could be home as early as ten, ten-thirty. Will that do?"

"Great!" He gave a short, decisive nod. "Yes, okay. Ten-thirty. They usually wrap up by ten. Bye for now."

He swivelled on his heel and left. Sunny saw him head for the cabin his father occupied.

Sunny stood where she was for a full moment, inwardly laughing at the great awkwardness of Grant in asking for the privacy the Prentiss clan needed.

Traditions!

She walked through the apartment to the deck. "Tracy...how would you like to go to dinner and a movie tonight?"

Chapter Sixteen

Sunny was tired when she and Tracy came home from town. Dell was still at work. It was almost 11:00 p.m. All was quiet down on the docks and in the swimming area. A light was on in cabin four; she guessed a last jawing crowd was there. She wondered how the swimming party had gone.

"Want anything Tracy?" she asked, turning on the office night light.

"No. Thanks for the movie, Sunny. It was a fun evening, but I think I'll go to bed now, if it's all right with you."

"Sure. You can have the bathroom first. I'm going to hit the sack soon myself."

As Tracy went into the apartment, Sunny switched on the light over the computer. She turned it on and checked tomorrow's reservations. Two, as she'd remembered.

She closed the screen. Next she hit the money drawer. She hadn't had time to check the cash today, but the amount should be the same as yesterday and the day before.

Without thought, she took out the bills and began to count, thinking she had to make a bank run soon. Then she stopped abruptly. There, on the bottom of the stack, was a fifty-dollar bill. Fifty dollars?

It was the amount she'd been short before. When was that? Two weeks ago? It had been returned.

Who had returned it? Dell sometimes worked in the office, but not lately. Not since the Prentiss family had come. He hadn't been there since he'd started his outside job—except for the couple of hours he'd taken his nap on the sofa. Tracy didn't have access to the drawer.

Oddly, she didn't believe it was Dell.

It was a puzzle. Had she overlooked the money when counting it the first time?

No…she didn't think so. Then who? Grant? He knew how the drawer worked. She'd left him alone when she had a quick errand for cabin two the other day.

Nah… Never Grant.

The water had ceased running in the bathroom by the time she made her way into the apartment. She closed the apartment door quietly and went straight to her bedroom, absently laying her purse on top of the dresser. Getting out her pajamas, she glanced at the books by her bedside, her Bible on top. She thought she'd read Hebrews tonight.

Hebrews talked of all the faith the Old Testament fellows had. They'd made their share of mistakes, yet Hebrews pointed out their great faith, faith that God would come through, and without it nothing was any good in life.

She sighed. She sure didn't know what God intended when He gave her this resort. Her life seemed to get more entangled every day.

Tracy came out of the bathroom, and went into the living area. "Mind if I have the TV on for a little while?"

"No, but please keep the sound low," Sunny replied. "And not too long. You need some sleep."

"Okay."

Sunny changed, then sat on the side of her bed. She opened her Bible to Hebrews. She read a couple of chapters, then lay back, putting her Bible back on her table.

She reached for the handful of photographs she'd kept out. Often, they were the last thing she looked at before she went to sleep. Snapshots of her grandmother and grandfather and her dad, Johnny.

She shuffled through them once more. Why couldn't she have known them? There was her grandmother Shirley, holding a yellow daisy. And her granddad, Nathan, standing on the docks.

Johnny stood by his bright red pickup, his hands in his front pockets, smiling widely into the camera lens. He appeared to be about eighteen.

She sighed once more and put the snapshots away.

The next morning one by one the Prentiss men left. Grant said a lingering goodbye to his dad and brothers, but at last let them go. Sunny watched from the office, but finally went outside to say goodbye. Grant and Sunny stood waving as first Gray pulled away, then his dad and Linc, the boat lumbering on its trailer.

"Well, that's it for this year," said Grant as they

drifted into the office. He pushed his baseball cap to the back of his head, while a note of wistfulness entered his voice.

"You miss them."

"Yep."

"If you miss them so much, maybe it would be better to move back to the city where you can see them more often." She hesitated to offer her advice, yet she couldn't help the thought.

"Nah." His gaze was soft. "I'd miss this place here. Besides, a man has to stand on his own." He prepared to leave, taking off his cap, brushing back his hair while he reasoned, "They're only three hours away. I can go visit any time I really want, like at Christmas."

She nodded, playing with a stack of papers on the counter. "Sure you can."

Like for Christmas and Thanksgiving. Easter and…

She turned away, wishing more than anything in the world she had family to visit. To buy presents for. To celebrate the high days in a person's life and listen during the valleys. The holidays were difficult; she didn't always have the Larsons to go to—sometimes they were occupied with their own families.

She usually worked on those days—making merry for the people who were hospitalized and to give married nurses the time off to be with their families. But privately, working gave her something to do with the days.

"Do you have any reservations today?" she asked to change the subject.

"Yeah, got a couple coming at ten. That's all, though." He turned in the doorway. "Hey, Sunny, why don't we go swimming tonight? It's supposed to be a nice evening."

"All right." Her heart lifted with excitement. "I suppose I should find out firsthand how the water is and if the accommodations are all right."

"Yeah, that's right. About seven?"

"Sure. That's fine."

"See you then."

The rest of the day seemed flat without the hubbub of men and boys. Dell took down his tent, and he and Tracy moved back into cabin one. Tracy seemed happy about it, and Sunny was, too. Yet after her work was complete, Tracy sat down at the dock and stared at the lake.

Sunny took Tracy with her into town and dropped her at her friend's house, with the promise that Dell would pick her up.

Then she made a speedy trip to the bank and grocery store so that she could shop. She needed a new bathing suit.

After shuffling through dozens of suits, she found a modest one piece in hot pink in only the second shop she visited. She held it up for inspection. It was rather plain, but it would do for lake swimming, she thought. She wasn't out to impress anybody.

Hah!

Thoughts of Grant's handsome smile immediately came to the forefront. It certainly tickled her fancy. Plus sometimes the way he looked at her was as soft and dreamy as a cloud.

She sighed, pushing thoughts of him once more into the back of her mind. She had other errands to do.

She was home just before noon, when another three men were due to check in. They arrived in a large pontoon boat about thirty minutes later and docked on the outside of the wooden structure. They had fishing gear to the max and talked of the latest fishing news.

Sunny was getting used to it.

Toward evening, Grant drove up and parked in the now neatly sectioned parking area. Sunny came out of the office, a short white terry bathrobe over her suit. She'd braided her long hair and pinned it on top of her head. It made her hazel eyes appear larger.

Grant studied her, his soft thoughts showing. He wore short cargo pants and a T-shirt; his old sneakers had holes and were dirty down into the seams. Had he worn them since high school?

"Ready?"

"Yeah," she said as a chuckle gurgled.

"What's so funny?"

"Your shoes. Don't you throw anything away?"

"Nah," he glanced down, inspecting his shoes, "they're good for the lake. You can't wear those sandals you have on, and you can't go barefoot. The beach is so rocky you'll cut your feet if you don't wear something on them. Haven't you got any old canvas sneakers or something?"

"Um…" she thought. What did she have? She'd found an old pair of tennis shoes in her grandfather's things, things she'd packed, but couldn't bring herself to throw away. "You go on down, I'll be there in a minute."

She went into the apartment and to the closet. On her knees, she searched the box until she came up with the shoes in question. They were grungy, and probably too big. She picked one up to smell it, twitching her nose.

The flip-flops! They'd do. She searched the bottom of the box, coming up with blue flip-flops. These would do just fine. They looked as if they hadn't been worn.

When she arrived at the swimming area, Grant was already in the water. He urged her in, and she quickly took off her robe and slippers and dove smoothly off the edge of the swimmers' dock and into the water.

Grant tagged her as she came up. "Forgot to ask. Are you a good swimmer?"

"Fair."

"Okay. See that barrel?" He pointed to the designated swimming limit. "I'll race you."

The barrel wasn't far, and she immediately took off, arm over arm. Behind her, she heard a strangled grunt. Grant reached the barrel first, but only by an arm's length.

"I won," he pronounced gleefully. They paused, treading water.

"Only because I haven't swum for ages," she challenged. "Let's try it again."

They raced two more lengths before they gave up and simply lolled on floating rubber rafts.

The sun, losing heat, was dipping below the horizon when they came out. The tall pole holding the night light came on; it wouldn't go off until midnight.

Two of her guests were just getting in from the lake, docking their boat as Sunny climbed from the lake. The men waved, but paid them no more attention.

Grant climbed out behind her in his navy swimsuit,

and she handed him a dark-green towel. The water lay gleaming, wet and shining along his brawny arms and legs. He brushed it away with the towel.

She glanced away, struggling to keep her composure. She couldn't let him see the admiration that overcame her. A finer-looking man didn't exist, she thought. Working that ranch must agree with him, she mused, building his muscles to perfection.

"That was great!" he said.

She swallowed. "Yes, I really enjoyed it."

"Are these new towels?"

"Mmm-hmm." She proceeded to towel off her arms, then her neck. "I bought them today. The ones in my bathroom are so thin you can see through them."

"They're nice." He studied the thick terrycloth. "You didn't have to buy them on my account."

"I didn't." She bent to dry her legs and feet, then slipped on the flip-flops once more. "I bought them on *my* account. I also bought a couple of new sets for bathroom use."

He sniffed the air. "Even the air feels cooler after an evening swim."

"Mmm…" She slipped her arms through her robe. He merely put on his shirt over his wet swimsuit. "I'm up for a cup of coffee, I think. Want one?"

"Sure."

Starting up the slope, she dropped her towel. She halted to pick it up, more in shadow than in the direct night light.

"Here, I'll get it," he said, bending for it. He gently placed the towel about her neck, carefully arranging the folds with slowing hands. His knuckles brushed the side of her neck, raising goose bumps along her skin.

She stared into his soft gaze, her thoughts beginning to scatter. She struggled to keep them together. Why did he affect her that way?

"That pink suits you," he murmured as his eyes grew softer. He leaned into her so naturally, it didn't seem like a play for her affection. It was simply Grant reaching for her. He laid his lips along her cheek, sliding until he reached her mouth. The kiss went on…and on…until she slowly eased away.

"I've wanted to kiss you all day," he muttered.

"You have?"

"You didn't know?"

"No. How could I?"

"Thought maybe you could read my mind." He kissed her again, his lips so soft she thought she'd float. She could barely breathe.

When she broke away, a lingering sweetness remained. She breathed deeply, catching his faint scent of aftershave. She retreated a step.

"I thought you wanted some coffee."

He smiled a slow entrancing smile. "I do. With cream and sugar."

She took another step backward, feeling tingly all over. She edged back another step. "Then let me get dressed. You sit on the deck, please."

"Okay." He followed her, a grin just at the edge of his mouth. "If you insist."

"I do insist." She nodded vigorously. "I can't make coffee if you're, um…"

"Guess I'll have to be good."

"Mmm-hmm..."

"All right. Change and make the coffee."

She wanted to run, but she simply hurried her pace. She was silly to be so happy over a kiss.

She started the small pot of water for instant coffee, then went into the bedroom to get dressed. Quickly getting into shorts and a T-shirt, she put the mugs and a dish of sugar cookies out on a tray, and carried them out.

Grant sat on the step, leaning against the post. The green towel lay folded beside him.

"Here we are," she said. That sounded silly, she thought. Obviously, there they were. But what else could she say?

The deck was dark; she hadn't turned on a light and the moon wasn't high yet. She sat on the opposite side of him as she handed him his mug. Taking a sip of her own coffee, listening to Grant munch on a cookie, she looked out at the night. The other cabins lay a short distance away, some dark, but two with lights.

Grant sipped, then murmured, "Thanks. This hits the spot."

After a moment he set his cup down, stretched his legs out, down the stairs, then brought his legs back under him to lazily stand.

"Gotta go. Have some work to do before morning."

"Oh, you do?" She rose, too, her palms feeling warmed by her cup.

"Wish I could stay." He placed his hand on her shoulder, rubbing his thumb against the side of her neck.

"Um...well..." she wished it, too. "You can't. But there's always tomorrow."

"Yeah, but tomorrow is very busy. Maybe tomorrow night, though. I'll need another swim, I think."

She laughed softly. "I'll see you tomorrow down at the swimming dock. About seven?"

"It's a date."

Sunny remained on the deck, watching Grant walk around the outside of her cabin to the parking area. She listened for the thrum of his motor and saw him drive down the road. She sighed at the day's ending; it had been perfect.

It was rather late; time for bed.

Yet when she entered the house, she suddenly paused. A raw unsettled feeling came over her. Why? What bothered her?

She gazed about the room. Things seemed to be in place. The coffee things were out, so she put them away. Then going into the bedroom, she saw things scattered from the box in which she'd found the flip-flops. She'd hurriedly left things out when she'd searched through it.

But she hadn't laid a thing on the bed. In years past, she'd often been teased about her need to keep her bed neatly made, and it was always, always straight. She hadn't messed with the old chenille cover.

Near the edge lay a wrinkle, as if someone had been sitting there. And beside it was a picture of her father when he was about sixteen. She hadn't placed it there.

Her heart began to pound. She didn't believe in ghosts. Did she?

Chapter Seventeen

Sunny approached the hospital with confidence. She had had to squeeze the time into her morning, but she'd thought she must. Tracy started school next week, and Sunny had to work around that schedule, but she was positive she could get in a few hours nursing. She'd take anything.

Her bills were piling high and her savings account wasn't strong enough to carry more debt at the moment. The new washer and dryer sat in the back corner of the garage, making everything around it look old. Nevertheless, she was proud of them. In spite of the bills, she was making progress.

Too bad the cabin rates were so low. Yet she couldn't see raising the rent when the cabins hadn't been improved for at least twenty years. But they covered her operating expenses, thank goodness. Actually, a small profit was beginning to show.

She parked Ol' Winnie, patting it to give her luck,

then entered the hospital. It was small. She had no trouble finding the personnel office. The woman at the desk glanced at her and gave her the application without saying much. She filled it out and thanked the woman, then left. They'd call her for an interview.

She planned to run by the grocery store, then home. She needed more food on hand with Dell and Tracy, she mused. The kids were beginning to take hold, and she was proud of them. Tracy became more comfortable as time went by, and Dell worked keeping the docks clean after his full-time job each day.

As she opened Ol' Winnie's door, she heard her name called. She turned to see Jim Lindberg approaching. She hadn't seen him since that first morning at church.

As usual, Jim wore a navy suit. She had yet to see him in casual clothes.

"Hi, Jim."

"Hi, Sunny. I've been meaning to call you. Been so busy with that new condo down on Holloway Street, I haven't had any time of my own to do anything. Boy, those condos are selling like hot cakes, let me tell you. They're priced too low, I'm thinking, but the builder simply wants to sell 'em and get his money out of 'em." He took a breath. "How have you been?"

"Fine. I'm glad to hear you're selling condos."

"Me, too. What have you been doing with yourself out at Sunshine Acres?"

"Taking care of the fishermen," she said with a chuckle.

"Ah, yes. That's the resort's stock in trade, isn't it?"

"Mmm-hmm. My grandfather has some steady customers. Some of those people have been coming to Sunshine Acres for years. They seem to want the place to stay the same."

She suddenly realized there was comfort to be drawn from that. They loved the resort, had loved her granddad. Maybe they didn't want the resort to change too much.

"Hmm…interesting. Say, I ran into your dad's old friend, Frankie Brewster, the other day."

"Who?"

"A fellow by the name of Frankie Brewster? Tall, skinny guy with brown hair? His face looks like a road map? The two used to be chummy." Sunny looked blank, prompting Jim to say finally, "You never heard of him?"

"No, I never knew any of my father's friends," she remarked. "Never knew my dad. He died before I was born."

"He did? Wow! I'm sorry, Sunny. Had you ever met your grandparents then?"

"No. Never."

"Aw, that's a bum deal. No wonder you seemed a bit stunned that first day. Look," he glanced at his watch "I have to run. But I'm going to call you soon for that lunch. Bye now."

"Bye…"

Sunny laughed as she climbed into the truck and turned the key. She doubted she'd ever get a call for a date until she called him to say she was ready to sell. But she didn't want a date with Jim Lindberg, did she?

She didn't think of Jim again until that night when she walked down to the lake for her swim. She and Grant had met almost every evening this last week.

Sometimes Tracy joined them, and one night a couple of guests did, too. The continuous activity was great fun and relaxing.

And she and Grant often had a few minutes alone.

At the moment, no one was there at the swimming dock. She sat on the flat wooden edge dangling her legs in the water until someone came. She took seriously the warning never to swim alone.

A tuneful whistling sounded behind her, and she turned to see Grant coming down the slope, his lips puckered. His expression lightened, and he ended the tune as a grin began when he spotted her.

"Waiting for me?"

"Waiting for anyone," she said and shrugged.

"Not just for *me?*"

"Now just what store would I put into waiting for you?" Resisting a smile, she gazed up and over her shoulder at him, raising an eyebrow.

"Not much, I guess." He teased as he threw down his towel, a white one he'd brought from home.

"Well, I'm glad you're here." She slid into the water at the same time he swiftly dove. It made a great splash and threw her off balance. She moved quickly, treading water, and suddenly took in a swallow of water. "Why, you—" she coughed.

She splashed water at him, but he swam away.

Swimming after him, she tagged the buoy just after he did and folded herself to turn. She pushed herself to catch him, swimming at his heels.

Grant hefted himself up, leaning his folded his arms along the dock until she reached the ladder.

"Hear that?" he questioned.

"What is it?" She listened to a low thrum which grew louder as they listened.

"It's a huge boat." He stretched to look, "And I think it's coming in here."

She hauled herself up on her arms to see over the dock. Sure enough, the boat that was heading their way was a monster.

"Better get out then." She climbed quickly out and donned her robe. She glanced out toward the main channel—the monster boat was coming toward her docks. "Oh, boy."

Sunny slipped her feet into the blue flip-flops and walked along the dock until she reached the outer edge. It was deeper water on this end, giving safe haven to such big boats. Three people stared at her from the boat. One of them was Jim Lindberg, waving.

"Hey, can we come alongside?"

"I suppose so. Come on ashore." Sunny couldn't help her politeness, but she wished Jim wouldn't bring people by to look at her property until next spring. Or without warning. The couple with Jim were staring at her eagerly.

"We were just passing your place and thought we'd stop by," Jim said, giving a glance at her long legs. The boat deck stood above her, forcing her to look up.

Behind her, she heard Grant snort. Chances of an offhand visit from the Realtor were about as possible as snow in August.

"Well, come on in and sit awhile," she offered.

"This is Mr. and Mrs. Hubbard, from St. Louis," Jim

introduced as the middle-aged, dark-haired couple disembarked. He introduced Sunny and Grant, mentioning Grant's Retreat as he did so.

"How do you do." She smiled a little tentatively. "We were just over at the swimming area."

Mrs. Hubbard jangled her gold bracelets as she stepped gingerly ashore. She smoothed down her expensive T-shirt and smiled politely at Sunny. But her interested eyes shifted to Grant, taking in his muscular chest.

The woman said nothing.

Sunny led them all to the sociable end of the dock.

Grant grabbed his shirt from where he'd thrown it on the dock and proceeded to put it on while Jim showed the Hubbards to the chairs. Sunny glanced at him from her peripheral vision, hoping his frown didn't mean he was about to leave. But he simply sat down on the deck.

"Nice weather," said Mr. Hubbard. He had only started to speak when Grant spoke.

"Supposed to rain by Sunday," put in Grant before the man could add anything.

"I think so. But we need rain, even though it puts a damper on lake activities," said Mr. Hubbard.

"It's supposed to clear by afternoon," said Jim.

"I hope so because I have a big group reserved. Fifteen riders." Grant cast a glance at Jim, then continued. "Going to take them on the longer trail. We cleared that underbrush all the way up to that peak in the distance. You can view the lake from there. It's a great spot and I'm thinking of making it a regular run for folks who want a complete ride and not just a scrap of one."

He paused for breath, and Sunny frowned at him.

What was he trying to do, talk them to death? Grant accepted her silent command and clamped his mouth closed, angry lines bracketing his mouth. He knew, she knew…that he wanted to buy that land.

In the pause that ensued, Jim flashed Grant a barely disguised glance of disgust. He then jumped in with "Mr. Hubbard is interested in real estate here at the lake, Sunny."

"Uh-huh. A regular developer," mumbled Grant.

Sunny ignored him. "Well, I—"

"Now I know you can't sell for a while yet," said Jim. But I thought—"

She interrupted, "Yes, but, Jim, I'm not in a position to even *think* about selling at the moment."

"No, no… You've the winter to get through," said Mr. Hubbard smoothly. His quick glance at Jim told her they'd discussed her situation already.

How dare he push her? Sudden resentment rose, and she realized she wasn't one hundred percent sure anymore about selling.

Mr. Hubbard continued. "But I'd like to look the place over, if you don't mind. See the possibilities. You've got deep water here, and I can see you've got a prime piece of real estate. I'd offer a good price."

"It's very kind of you, Mr. Hubbard," she said, trying to keep her stiffness at bay, "but I'm not prepared to show the place at this time. And I won't be ready until late next spring." Very late. "I'll call you when I think the time is right. But I can't—I *won't* make a decision now."

"Yes, I see." Mr. Hubbard rose, pulling his gold card case from him pocket. "Take my card, please. Keep it, don't throw it away. I'll be around."

She accepted the card Mr. Hubbard handed her.

"I think a horseback ride would be lovely, don't you, Sanford?" Mrs. Hubbard spoke, indicating Grant. "We should take one, see how safe it is. After all, we can't recommend it to our associates unless we know about it."

"True, sweetie pie," Mr. Hubbard muttered "but I don't have time right now. Maybe in the fall…"

"Uh, be seeing you, Sunny," Jim said as he ushered the Hubbards back on their boat.

"Sure, Jim." Grant spoke jovially. "You all take care now."

As the boat pulled away, she turned to scold Grant for his rude behavior. "Now why—"

She noticed the couple from cabin four had come down to view the boat and were standing at the top of the concrete steps. She clamped her mouth shut.

"That was quite a boat," called the older man.

"Yes, it was," Sunny raised her voice to reply.

"Ha! Dodged that one." Grant said underneath his breath, looking pleased with himself.

"You think so?" Sunny muttered for his ears as the couple turned away.

"Think I'll be going now." Grant picked up his towel. "Got work to do."

"Yes, run away, why don't you?" Her hands went to her hips.

His grin went lopsided, and he leaned in to kiss her. It was swift but hard for just one moment and felt… wonderful. "Tomorrow?"

He strolled away while she stood still. Her mouth

was throbbing from the impression of his, and her ears
buzzed with his murmur of promise.

She wanted to scream.

"Sunny, I've got an evening ride lined up for Friday
night. Want to come?"

Her frustration forgotten, Sunny held the phone
closer to her ear. Tracy started school this morning, and
Sunny had driven her to the bus stop because Dell's
work schedule didn't allow him to take her. Her own
schedule was becoming complicated.

Grant asked the question nonchalantly, so she answered in a similar way. "Sure. What time?"

"About five-thirty. The trail will be light until about
seven, so we'll be back about then. Then we'll have a
wienie roast after. Buzz will provide biscuits and vegetables. Got all tin dishes last week for it, and a big
coffeepot, which we'll use for hot chocolate. Think
it'll work?"

"I think that will be fun. Who's coming?"

"Some young people from the church, would you
believe?"

"Really?" She hadn't realized he'd made that much
contact at the church. She warmed to the project. "Oh,
that's great. Then Tracy can come, too, and Dell?"

There wasn't even a hesitation in his voice these days
when a matter concerned Tracy and Dell. "Sure, bring
'em. Can't hurt. Hey, Sunny…"

"Yes?"

"Um, Buzz will need a little help with the serving and
stuff. I'll be guiding the kids, then taking care of the

horses. I wondered if you could…I mean, would you be willing to help out?"

The idea bloomed with possibilities, Sunny thought. How wonderful to give the area kids a treat! Perhaps they could give foster kids a special evening, too. Foster kids and even special-needs kids appreciated those things. They had no chance at them unless given as a gift. A ride and outdoor dinner as a treat? You bet!

The idea excited her as she dreamed.

Perhaps even the Larsons might come down for a vacation, she mused. Why hadn't she thought of it before? She could offer free lodging for a week…and a horseback ride? They could swim every day and hike. All it would cost them would be the gas to come down. It would be a wonderful experience for them all.

"Sunny?"

"Oh, uh, sure, Grant," she replied with warmth. "I'll help any way I can."

"It's a date then. I'll tell Buzz you're on board."

Chapter Eighteen

On Friday afternoon, Sunny arrived at Grant's Retreat early. She'd seen a horse trailer go down the road earlier, which made her wonder, *How big was this outing?*

Handling a crowd for dinner, she knew about, though she'd never cooked for one. In the Larsons' household, dinner often involved ten or twelve mouths to feed. Twenty wouldn't be a stretch.

"Thought we'd serve from this spot." Grant said. He wore his Western gear, his hat tipped to the back of his head, and Sunny, gazing at him, wanted to melt.

He hadn't a clue to how effective he appeared, she thought. Like a movie-star cowboy from the old days, strong and in charge. He was concentrating on his big night.

Lord, I'm getting as mushy as a cream pie left to an August sun. Help me, please?

She had to be practical, she scolded herself.

They stood at the back end of the corral where Grant

had directed them to. Sunny had never been in this area of the ranch before. The ground here was fairly level next to the horseshoe court. He'd cleared a large circle of weeds, and in the middle set a campfire, surrounded with stones. Two wooden tables stood to one side. They looked new.

"We can drive the truck right up here," he said pointing to the already parked truck, "and use the truck bed for serving, too. We're just going to have hot dogs and baked potatoes tonight. Buzz already has those in the oven, but he can bring them out later. And toppings, of course. We'll see how it goes for the first time."

"Great. That'll do for the kids. Do you have plastic tablecloths?"

"Buzz?" Grant turned to his helper.

The man glanced up, then said in his gruff way, "I don't handle the buyin' end of things."

"Okay," she soothed. "You don't have time to go into town to buy them. Can we use newspaper?"

"That'll do," Grant said, relieved. "I'll go to the house for some. You see if we need anything else."

Sunny started looking through the supplies in the boxes in the truck. She pulled out brand-new tin plates, cups and inexpensive flatware. An aged iron pot that she supposed Buzz would use in the future sat on the ground near the truck. Hot dogs and buns, relish, mustard, ketchup and a can of sauerkraut sat next to a thirty-cup coffeepot that looked brand new. A capped tub of cocoa mix was next to it. There were many supplies: butter and cheese for the potatoes, paper napkins, salt and pepper, a five-gallon cask of water, marshmallows, graham crackers and chocolate bars. It would take a little time to set it all out.

Grant returned with the newspaper, and Sunny spread it over the picnic tables, taping it down with the tape Grant brought out.

"Gotta go tend to the horses now. Saddle up." He turned to look at all the fixings for supper. "Guess we have everything."

He started away, but turned again. "Dell's coming, isn't he?"

"Yes, he's coming along," Sunny replied.

"Good."

When Grant left, she quickly set everything out. When it was done, she stepped back to view it. It looked divine, she thought.

She heard the bus before it arrived. Dust puffed up, stirring the gravel road. And the kids were singing.

They got off chattering, and remained noisily excited. Grant suddenly appeared and spoke to their leader, a young man with curly hair and glasses who was their youth minister, a man named Thad. They all lined up around the corral, looking at the horses, pointing eagerly to the showy ones.

"People!" Grant shouted to be heard over the hubbub.

Then all grew quiet while Grant gave his newcomers' speech.

"Hello. I'm glad you've chosen to come to Grant's Retreat for an outing. We aim to give you a happy ride, and later a wienie roast. Now there's eighteen of you, aren't there?"

While Grant was giving directions, Dell and Tracy

arrived. Dell parked next to the bus and they got out. Having ridden before, Tracy proudly acted like an old hand. She lounged against the corral post with a casualness that was a bit comical, considering how nervous she'd been before.

"Dell!" called Grant. He glanced their way.

"Yeah?" Dell poked his head over the top rail of the corral.

"Want to give me a hand?"

"Sure, Grant." He quickly ducked through the corral fence and idled up to Grant, who was adjusting stirrups.

"As each rider mounts, we need to check the stirrup lengths. Think you can you handle that?"

"Yeah, sure." Dell flashed his eyes at Grant, then at his sister.

Sunny ambled up to the fence where Tracy stood. "How's it going?"

"Fine."

Grant seemed not to notice them until he suddenly called her. "Tracy…"

"Uh-huh?" The girl swiftly looked up, her eyes round as a night owl's. Grant beckoned.

"Will you come and show the proper way to mount?"

Surprise flickered across Tracy's face, but she quickly straightened to cover the emotion. Stepping forward eagerly, she showed not one ounce of the fear she'd shown before. Sunny noticed Grant had Coyote ready. Coyote turned her head, as though to welcome Tracy.

Sunny let go of a long breath she hadn't known she held. Her hand tightened on the top rail.

Nearby, Dell was shortening the stirrups on one of

the mounts. He glanced up anxiously at Grant's directive; his hands slowed as he watched his sister mount in a perfect swing. He ducked his head and gave a slow smile, saying under his breath, "Good job."

"Now I'm counting on you to help trail these church kids," he told Tracy in a low tone. "Some of these kids have experience, but not all of them. Dell will bring up the absolute tail. Sunny's going to stay and help Buzz."

Tracy took the lead easily, and then came the long line of kids. Twenty of them, one by one, counting Dell and Tracy. Dell trailed them all, watching for anyone who might be having a problem.

Where had Grant gotten the extra horses to mount them all? She recalled the heavy horse trailer she'd seen earlier. He must have rented some of the mounts.

Sunny stood as they trailed out, and she watched them all the way until they disappeared up the woody slope. It struck her as a beautiful sight. The sun was low, giving long shadows, and she suddenly wished she'd brought a camera.

"Buzz, do you have a camera I can borrow?"

"Hmm, reckon you can borrow Grant's. It takes good shots."

"That's what I want," she told him.

He fetched it, and she was thankful it already had film in it. Then while Buzz built a fire, she opened hot dogs and buns, pickles and relish.

An hour later, the sun was sinking in long slow decline as the riders came up the meadow. Some of the kids were singing, and Sunny could tell by their expressions how much they liked the experience. They would come again.

They came into the corral, Buzz ready to help them dismount, and some wobbled over to the campfire.

"I'm starved," said one girl, petite and pretty.

"Where's the rest room?" whispered another into Tracy's ear. Tracy pointed toward the barn. "Here, I'll show you." Tracy led the way into the barn, where a rest room was stationed.

Sunny noticed Dell helping some of the older teen girls to dismount, flirting as he did. Then he proceeded to help Grant unsaddle the horses, while the kids gathered around the campfire.

"This has been a great outing, hasn't it, gang?" The youth minister spoke and the kids grew quiet. "Let's ask the Lord's blessings before we eat."

The sheep hear their master's voice… Sunny thought idly. Yet it was true of her as well. She bowed her head.

"Oh, Lord, we've enjoyed our ride out here at Grant's Retreat tonight. We thank You for it, and ask Your blessings on Grant and on his stable. Now we're provided with a great supper, so we thank You for that, too. We pray in Your name, Amen."

Sunny busily passed the long forks and sticks Grant had whittled especially for the hot dogs. The kids grabbed them and skewered hot dogs in a flash.

Buzz busily poured potatoes into a long dish and set a bowl of grated cheese and butter beside it.

A couple of the boys laughingly broke into swordplay, brandishing their sticks in mock battle.

"Now, guys, stop that," she heard herself say. "Those sticks are sharp. Someone might get hurt."

She was about to caution the boys further when she

heard, "Ouch, ouch, ouch!" and a little girl put a finger up to her mouth. Sunny dropped the package of buns she held and hurried around the circle.

"Here, sweetie, let me see it," she told the young girl, holding out her hand in invitation. The girl extended her small brown hand to view. A nasty cut began to bleed from the girl's forefinger. Sunny made her voice personal. "Ah, it's not too bad. What's your name?"

"Courtney," came the reply.

"Buzz!" Sunny raised her voice to call the older man. She noticed Tracy take over passing out things as she attended to the small emergency.

"Yeah?" Buzz answered.

"Have you got a first aid kit?"

"Sure do. I'll get it."

"Nothing to worry about, hon," Sunny soothed as Buzz came around the campfire with the kit in hand. "It's only a small cut. You can have a hot dog after we clean this."

The youth minister stood nearby, concern on his face, as Sunny dabbed the cut with a swab. "Are you all right, Courtney?"

"Uh-huh. I caught my finger on something. It's nothing. Miss Sunny is getting me a Band-Aid."

"That's good," Thad mumbled.

The kids ate hot dogs and some roasted potatoes, and then they toasted marshmallows until none were left. A short boy with bright brown eyes started strumming his guitar, and Sunny marveled at how alike church youth groups were everywhere. Many of the kids curled down on the ground, singing or listening, while others milled about looking at things on the ranch. Sunny looked up and realized suddenly that dark had fallen.

The party broke up around nine, and the youth minister herded all the kids onto a bus.

"Bye, Tracy. Bye, Miss Sunny. See you at church," called Courtney.

"Bye, Tracy. See you at school," called the girl Tracy had befriended. Tracy smiled and waved; she appeared so pleased to make new friends a person could hang a certainty that it was true.

Sunny thought of Tracy and her situation as she helped Buzz and Tracy pick up the remains of food and trash. With God's help, maybe this year wouldn't be so tough after all.

"Any hot dogs left?" asked Grant, coming forward out of the dark. He'd finished unsaddling at last and had turned the horses into the pasture. Dell came trailing behind. "Dell and I could sure eat a couple."

"Buns left. But hot dogs, uh-uh. Hafta get another package out of the fridge," Buzz said. He trotted around the corral and headed toward the house.

"We appreciate it." Grant hunched down by the fire and held out his palms toward it. "We underestimated the amount they'd eat, I guess. How many kids were here? Forgot what a healthy appetite a teenager has."

Dell squatted beside Grant. "Eighteen, not counting Tracy," he said with a smile. "Good number. Sure am hungry."

The men talked in low tones as Sunny and Tracy picked up tin cups and plates and piled them into a washtub.

"Grant, that was a very nice thing to do. The kids will remember what a good time they had." Sunny talked as she put the lid back on the pickles. Her dream of offering foster kids a similar experience had climbed ten times. Foster kids did better in school and socially if they had the same opportunities as other kids.

"I was glad to do it, really. But I had an ulterior motive for having the party. I wanted to know how to handle things, what the campfire could offer. Think I'll be able to plan a little better now that I've done it."

Buzz returned with a new package of hot dogs, and the two men skewered a few and put them over the now low coals. Sunny got out buns, and dipped sauerkraut.

"Oh, so it was selfishly done, was it?" she said, tongue in cheek. "Like I believe that!"

"It's true. I'm just a selfish son of a sweet mother, that's all."

"Uh-huh." Obviously, she didn't believe him.

Dell gave a chuckle, but didn't add his opinion.

Grant accepted his bun with a glance of appreciation, his eyes warm, while Tracy made sure Dell had what he wanted. Glancing around the campfire, he nodded. "Yeah, it'll work," he planned out loud, his mouth around his hot dog. "Gotta get a chuck wagon, I think. Looks better. More authentic."

"I've seen one down around Springfield," Dell said. "If they haven't sold the thing already."

"That kid with the music," continued Grant.

"Uh-huh. Nice touch," agreed Dell.

"I think his name is Nick," offered Tracy.

All at once, Sunny laughed out of sheer joy.

"What's so funny?" Grant turned to ask, his brow raised.

"Nothing. Nothing at all."

But it was enlightenment, true and sweet, after all. Truly, God had answered some of her prayers. Grant was getting along with Tracy and Dell just great.

By Friday, Grant had flyers out. He dropped a few at Sunny's desk, talking about how Dell had offered to drive down to Springfield with him to see that chuck wagon.

"We're going on Tuesday afternoon just as soon as he gets off work. I've offered him a job—"

"You have?" Sunny wasn't as surprised as she would've been two months earlier.

"I can't take him on full-time as yet. The winters are too slow."

"I'm sure Dell will be happy with anything. He seemed to really take to the horses, didn't he?"

"Yeah, he did. I'm thinking I can use him next year full-time."

Sunny hid her amusement. Grant had really changed his mind about Dell. Perhaps the kids could live with Grant at the ranch next year?

That brought her down with a jolt. All these plans going strong when she wouldn't be a part of them.

Chapter Nineteen

The kids from Three Corners Community Church greeted Tracy on Sunday with a happy welcome. Two girls that Sunny remembered from Friday night asked if Tracy would sit with them, and the girl disappeared down the aisle throwing a grin and "I'll see you later" over her shoulder.

A couple of boys from Friday's ride greeted Grant, too, when he took his seat beside her. Dell slipped into the pew just behind, and Sunny turned to give him a wide smile.

Thad, the youth minister, stopped by to speak to them, acknowledging Dell in the greeting, being friendly to all of them. He thanked Grant for his generosity once more. Sunny felt like an overly proud mother.

The pastor spoke of the many names of God in his sermon, and the enormity of what those names meant. The names were precious. Sunny had never before heard them all together, and she listened with fascination. *El-ohim...Jehovah...El Shaddai...Adonai...*

There were more, and the pastor announced he'd be preaching on one name a week until they'd studied all. It would take them almost to Christmas.

"That's an awesome line-up," said Grant as they were filing out of the sanctuary.

"Sure is…I don't want to miss a single one," Sunny answered dreamily. "Imagine, all those names mean something, they have an almighty power. But I should get home. There's two groups checking in around noon."

"Yeah, I've got people this afternoon, too. How about a swim after supper?" He leaned closer to her ear. "I've grown fond of our good-nights."

His breath on her neck sent a warm tingle down her limbs. She caught her breath. Their kisses on saying good-night were growing more intense. Sunny couldn't resist the promise.

"You're on."

A few moments past noon the two parties came in, asking about the fishing and about the swimming. A disappointment crept up her spine. If these folks were swimmers, that would put an end to her and Grant's privacy.

Ah, well. She was in business to give these folks a good vacation and the roped-off swim area was primarily for them.

"I hear there's a good fishing spot by that bluff south of here, but I can't vouch for it personally. And the swimming has been wonderful," she said, handing the middle-aged man the keys to cabin four. His youngish wife looked like the tomboy type. "The water is growing a little cooler now, but you can still swim. I hope you'll enjoy it."

After check-in, the place grew quiet once more. Grant's Retreat had a reservation for a party of five at one, and a party of six at three, Grant had told her. But they'd have their time together, and Sunny counted the hours until then.

Sunny's disappointment was realized when the older couple joined them in using the swimming area. But Grant seemed preoccupied about something and was rather quiet.

"Sorry, Sunny. I've got to cut this short tonight." He climbed out of the water and started to dry off. "Got stuff to do."

"Oh... Well, business first." Leaning against the ladder, she glanced at the older couple. They were within earshot.

Grant pulled his jeans on over his wet suit. He glanced at Sunny with a speculative softness as he buttoned his shirt, his eyes telling her he wanted nothing more than to have some private time with her. "See you."

She pressed her lips together, nodding. She watched him walk away and up the concrete steps.

It was obvious the couple were staying down here for the evening, but the lake no longer held her interest. Sunny got out of the water, smiling her professional smile as she grabbed her towel, and told the people "have a good time" as she strolled up to her cabin.

Monday was busy, as usual. About ten in the morning, the laundry service called to tell her they couldn't pick up her laundry—they'd trouble with their truck. Annoyed, Sunny tapped the counter, thinking rapidly, then said she'd bring the laundry in herself, and pick up her clean sheets and towels sometime in the afternoon.

She'd wait for Tracy. She was finding that having Tracy on call was a good thing. The girl more than made up for the lost rental to Sunshine Acres.

"Tracy, would you look after the office for a bit," Sunny asked as soon as Tracy got off the school bus. Sunny picked her up each day from the stop, hating to let Tracy walk the long distance to the resort on the rough gravel road. She'd been informed she could have the bus travel down to Sunshine Acres to pick up Tracy, but she hadn't yet made the call. "The laundry truck broke down and I've got to go pick up my sheets."

"Sure, Sunny."

She let Tracy out at the office and turned around to drive into town. Needing fresh air, she rolled down her window about halfway; the dust on the gravel kicked up too much for her to open it all the way. The dirty laundry basket was piled in the truck bed.

"Sunny…?" Tracy called her from the open office door.

What now? She hit her brake and rolled down her window further.

"Yeah?"

"Grant's on the phone. He—"

"Tell him I'll call him later."

"No, Sunny! It's an emergency… He wants you to come right on down to the ranch. Someone's hurt."

"Get my kit, Tracy." She had a few emergency aids in a box in the office.

Tracy came running to the truck, kit in hand, and Sunny accepted it through the window.

"Did they say what kind of accident it was?" Sunny asked, trying to hide her anxiety. She bit her lip; it wasn't Grant who was hurt...he'd made the call.

But it could be, she worried. What could've happened?

"No. They only said to hurry."

She drove as swiftly as she could on the gravel, then pulled to a quick stop in front of Grant's house. Grant rushed out from the barn, calling, "Down here, Sunny."

Sunny put the truck in gear, and drove the extra distance.

He met her halfway and grabbed her elbow with the strength she had come to expect from him. Sunny let her relief settle as she followed Grant with long strides. She found herself almost running to keep up with him.

"What happened?"

"A fall. The stupid, ignorant old—" Grant muttered.

"Is he conscious?"

"Yeah, and yelling at the top of his lungs about the need to lie flat until you could get here. Buzz heard him fall, so I left Buzz to sit on him."

Sunny could hear two male voices in argument, which grew louder as they turned the corner into the barn.

She listened to Grant, still muttering as they entered. "Why does he think he can do everything? He was trying to climb that ladder at the rear of the barn. With that bad knee acting up, too. He should know better. Wouldn't you think he'd use his brain for something beside holding his cap? What he was after, only God knows."

Sunny approached the scene with her professional

manner in place. A man lay on the floor, amid bits of hay. Buzz bent over the prone figure, his hands firmly on the man's shoulders.

"I'm *hurting,* I tell you." The salt-and-pepper hair needed cutting and heavy whiskers lined the man's jaw. His head rolled back and forth, his lined face twisted in agony. Droplets of sweat stood out on his brow. "The blasted thing hurts like blazes. Let me up so I can get somethin' to take."

Was the man in shock? Or did he always go on this way?

"Now I ain't agonna do it! You got to lay still."

The old man's hand brushed his face, then fell back on the straw where he lay. "I don't see why. I'm not unconscious, am I?"

"No, but you might of hurt something somewhere."

"I did, you nitwit!" His head came up in anger, his face wrenched with pain. He wore an old gray sweatshirt, which made his skin appear gray, and jeans. "I fell on my bad knee."

"I know that." Buzz held his ground with sympathy. "But you fell a piece, and we don't know how far. Gotta see if you're hurt anywhere else."

Sunny went to her knees to assess the problem. Then she caught her breath at the familiar face. An odd, eerie feeling crept up her spine as stared at the old man. She knew this man…

Her heart nearly broke as she realized who he was. Once, she'd seen his back from her office window as he'd visited with friends.

She'd met him in snapshots, traced his features with

her finger.... She'd almost caught him half a dozen times in the night when he'd visited her. At least, she presumed she'd almost caught him. It would explain the odd little happenings around her.

She'd read his Westerns, knew his handwriting, eaten at his table...

Nathan Merrill...her grandfather.

She reached out a hand to touch his cheek as mist gathered in her eyes. His skin felt cool enough.

Her thoughts tumbled about like clothes in the dryer, touching one fact after another in what she knew of him. She thought of all the intricate and broad matters she'd needed help on since her childhood.

Where had he been?

He stilled, staring at her, his mouth slack. "Sunny..." His croak drew the name out, watching her as she snapped to attention. Her name from his lips held a mountain of respect and longing.

"Lie still while I examine you," she commanded through her tight throat. A million questions tumbled about her mind. A million and one...

He said nothing while she proceeded to feel along his limbs, ascertaining the strength of his bones. Her touch became especially tender as she felt along his fractured leg with a butterfly touch. The bone was broken, but not through the skin. While her thoughts took in his condition, her anger at Grant grew to white heat.

Grant knew her grandfather was alive. He'd known all along.

Her glance flew to Grant's face, letting him see her anger. He returned her gaze for about two seconds before his skittered away. His mouth went firm, as though to hide his guilt.

Yes, he'd known the truth all along. While they'd played together and kissed so sweetly.

A pain so sharp she thought it rivaled any she'd ever felt centered around her heart.

Why had he kept the news from her? Why had Nathan? Were they playing with her emotions? Did they think this a joke?

"Have you called an ambulance?" she asked, still through a froggy throat.

"No, we called you first," Buzz answered.

"Get one on the way, please."

"I've called them, but I'll call again," Grant said.

Grant walked to the wide barn door where his voice could be heard talking with whoever was on the hospital emergency desk. He snapped his cell phone closed, and walked back to her. "They're on their way. It'll take…" his eyes flashed Nathan's way "a bit of time for them to get here."

"Get a pillow and a blanket," she instructed.

Buzz rose and left, on a quick run.

Her grandfather's hand crept out to latch on to hers. His fingers were warm and work-rough. He was quiet now. He continued to stare at her, taking in her features in minute detail. She turned her hand in his, holding it gently.

She spoke to Grant, holding her granddad's gaze. "Do you have a board or something I can use to stabilize his leg?"

Watching her grandfather's eyes follow her as she

worked, she gave a brief smile, trying to reassure him. His eyes glinted in return.

Then she took the clean board Grant had rummaged from somewhere in the back. She worked as gently as she could, placing the board under his leg.

"Yes, Granddad," she murmured when the old man groaned, closing his eyes a moment. "I know…I know you're in pain. We'll get you help just as soon as we can. The medics will be here soon."

Nathan's hand tightened on hers and he opened his eyes to look at her again. He opened his mouth as if he wanted to speak.

Sunny didn't want him to, not now. She wanted no explanations when he was hurt and in pain. She wanted them when he was well and healthy, when they would make some sense. She couldn't read his expression now.

"No, I won't leave you. Grant," she spoke smoothly as she turned her attention to Grant. "I'll need your belt, too."

Grant stripped it off immediately, while she crooned to Nathan. "You'll be fine in no time, you know? And those fishermen…they want to hear where the best places are to fish. They've been asking about you…"

Buzz came back with the pillow and blanket. She gently tucked them in place. "Now rest easy…no talking, just take it easy."

A very long thirty minutes passed while they waited. Sunny continued to watch Nathan's face. He didn't speak, but held her hand. She noted his fingers slowly relax as time went on; she thought he dozed lightly. They heard the ambulance approach, and Buzz went out to motion the medics down to the barn.

Two men came in, and Sunny reluctantly let go of Nathan's hand. They began a quick examination.

"Now you boys take it easy, here." Nathan awoke and started complaining as soon as they touched him. "I have a bum knee as it is, y'know. Ol' Doc has been after me about a knee replacement, but I put him off. Don't go jerky with me."

"No, we won't, Mr. Merrill. You take it easy now." One of the men spoke as they eased the old man onto a stretcher. "On three…" said the taller of the two. They carried Nathan out to the ambulance.

"My granddaughter…?" Nathan raised his head to look wildly about him. He held out his hand, and she rushed to put hers in it.

"Gentlemen…I am an R.N. I might be useful." Sunny pleaded with the shorter of the two. "Can I go with you? With him?"

"Sure, okay," the man nodded. "Climb in there, and we'll be on our way."

Sunny climbed into the ambulance, Nathan again reaching for her hand, and they started their trip to the county hospital.

The hospital kept Nathan all night. He was more comfortable that way. Sunny left him there, returning to Sunshine Acres with an aching heart, and with Grant.

But she was silent all the while. All the way home she thought of his deception. How could Grant lie to her?

Was this her home? That was one of a million questions she had for Nathan. And where would she put Nathan when he was released from the hospital?

"Sunny…we need to talk." Grant said the words as he pulled into Sunshine Acres' parking space.

"Not now, Grant." She turned toward the door.

"I don't think we should put it off." He braked the truck as she pushed the door handle.

"I doubt we have much to say." The door flung wide.

"We have a bunch of things to get straight between us."

Tracy came out of the office. "Is everything all right? I've been so worried since you called."

"Everything's fine, Tracy." Sunny slid out of the truck. It was almost dark. Where had the day gone? "But I'm exhausted now. Mind if we don't have supper together?"

She only wanted to climb into bed.

"Sunny…?" Grant pushed opened his door.

"No!" She flashed him an accusing glance. "I—I can't discuss anything right now. My grandfather is *alive*."

Her unspoken demand that he tell her it wasn't true, that there was some mistake in all this, that he hadn't lied to her, that nothing was what it seemed, stood starkly between them. She waited for the truth.

But he fell silent, while his face lost color, while his eyes looked as miserable as her banged-up heart. She turned away and whispered, "That's enough for the moment."

She flung into the office, leaving Grant to cope on his own, going through to her living quarters. She stopped suddenly by the bed, her heart feeling as though it had been put through a shredder. She wanted to cry and the tears clogged her throat.

She heard him leave and was glad of it. He could go…she didn't want anything more from him.

She was on her own again. Alone. And now she had a grandfather to deal with.

Her heart and thoughts were in chaos. But it was the disappointment in Grant that hammered the hardest at her battered spirit. She wanted to cry out, but the need to appear in control kept her quiet. She kept her eyes downcast to hide her tears.

Oh, Lord, I need You now.

Chapter Twenty

Early the next morning, Sunny went to see her grandfather. She had slept little, and she prayed as she drove into town.

Please Lord… Please… Let me be happy about finding my grandfather alive. I never knew…well, I didn't know. Help me to view him with a—a favorable…no, I don't mean that, I do see him as a positive factor in my life, I just wish…

After she parked Ol' Winnie, she brushed her hands over her eyes. *Oh, help me, please…I'm so confused about Grant, and what's going on.*

Grant! That dirty-dealing, no good rat!

She pushed open her door and got out, shoving those feelings down. She wouldn't feel so out of control, she just wouldn't.

Last night she'd been too tired to call Jessica, to ask for her advice. Even too dispirited, she mused. Besides, she no longer needed to depend on Jessica and Mark.

She didn't need anyone's advice except the Lord's. Of course there was an explanation for all this secrecy…she just hadn't found it yet.

The hospital was familiar in the way that all hospitals were alike, comforting her in with its sameness. She breathed deeply of its odors.

"Nathan Merrill?" she asked the information desk.

"Room two-fifteen."

"Thank you."

Not waiting for the elevator, she marched up the stairs. She glanced at the directional arrows on the wall, found two-fifteen, and walked into the room.

Nathan was arguing with the nurse.

"I tell you, I'm going home today." He pulled up on the overhead bar. "A broken leg won't keep me in the hospital. I've got work to do, woman. Now give me my pants."

"No doubt you can go home, Mr. Merrill, but the doctor hasn't signed you out yet. You'll have to stay until he can check you over."

"Don't see why I can't get dressed."

"I doubt your pants will fit over that cast. Can you call someone to bring you something to wear?"

Her cue, Sunny thought. "I'll see to him, nurse."

"Good luck," the young woman said under her breath as she left the room.

Sunny took a deep breath. She eased into the one chair beside his bed, saying calmly, "Well, now, Grandfather… Do you think the doctor will really let you go today?"

Nathan stared at her. "He will if he knows what's good for him. When he gets here. How are you, Sunny girl?"

"I'm fine." What a fib. "Just fine. And what can you wear?"

"That's good." He nodded. "I called Grant to bring me my robe." He tipped his head at her.

"Grant's coming?" she said, her eyebrows coming together. She didn't yet know how to treat Grant. As an enemy or friend? Yet he hadn't been a friend, quite. But he was no longer the tender almost-boyfriend whose eyes of blue could turn her heart to mush…and already she sharply missed that Grant. The attentive one, the playful one with whom she shared occasional meals, who teased her out of her loneliness.

"Yep. Any minute now."

"Maybe I'll just see about your breakfast…"

She rose and swivelled on her heel to head for the door, but came to an abrupt stop. Grant stood there. She bit her lip, and turned back to her grandfather.

"Well, he's here now," she said. She wandered to the window and stared out, ignoring Grant as best she could.

"Hi," she heard Grant say. "How are you feeling?"

"Not too bad at the moment. They had to put some pins in the leg. Got the ol' system full of pain killers. Ready to go home soon's the doc comes along to dismiss me."

The question arose in Sunny's mind once more: where did Nathan expect to go? Or after all this time, was it she who would go…back to Minneapolis?

Going back to Minneapolis had been growing in her mind. She had no job and no apartment there… But what could be accomplished in staying?

Except she had Nathan now. She couldn't leave. That

meant…that meant she'd see Grant every day? The lying son of a mud-speckled lake monster…

"I—I, um, I'll be back in a little while," she said, marching out of the room. She was so mad she thought the hospital walls were bright red.

When she reached the nurses' station, she stopped.

"When is Dr. Davis expected to make his rounds?" she asked. Dr. Davis was the doctor she'd met last night when they brought Granddad in.

"Around eleven," said the nurse, looking up from her computer.

"Thanks." Sunny walked the corridor with swift strides. She went down to the lobby, perused the gift shop, bought a bright red ball cap with a lake logo on it, and generally killed a half hour. She hoped Grant had gone home—she'd given him enough time.

But his bright blue eyes were the first thing she saw when she returned to her grandfather's room.

She quickly averted her gaze.

"Granddad, I thought you could use a new cap," she said, and brought the cap from the sack.

"By gum, I could at that." He reached for it, handling it with interest. "Nice of you, Sunny."

"Wouldn't you like to get cleaned up this morning? Before the doctor gets here?" She thought the nurses' assistant hadn't been around yet. "You'd be all ready to go then."

"Yeah, sure. Guess that'll take some time. Call the nurse."

"You forget, Granddad, *I'm* a nurse."

Grant remained quiet, watching the scene.

"Oh, but...I'd feel kinda funny with you helping me. I'll call the nurse."

"All right." Anything he wanted. "I'll wait outside."

She called the nurse, then turned to leave.

"Sunny..."

"Why don't you go home, now, Grant?" She was holding herself together by sheer will power. "You can't be of help any longer."

His gaze looked wounded, but he thrust out his jaw a moment. "I didn't want...I need to talk to you."

She dropped her gaze. "I don't think there's anything to talk about...now."

He stepped in front of her, blocking her against the hall wall.

"There is a great deal to talk about," he said harshly. "To clear up. Let me say it, Sunny."

She pushed him away, and disappeared into the ladies' room.

A few days later, all was quiet when she parked Ol' Winnie as close to the office of Sunshine Acres as she could. "Here we are, Granddad. Now just wait a minute till I can get your crutches."

She spotted Grant's truck at the far end of the parking space, and she stopped a moment.

"Sunny?" called her granddad.

"Coming." She held her temper in tight control.

She hurried around the truck, picking up the crutches as she went. Helping her granddad was her primary effort right now. He and Grant were friends. It was natural Grant would be on hand to see how her granddad got on. She wouldn't worry.

She'd only fume.

She spoke in a calm, even voice. "Let's get you comfortable, and then I'll prepare some lunch."

"The terrain is a lot smoother at the ranch." Grant suddenly appeared at their side. "It would be easier for you to come straight there."

"Unh…that is true," said Nathan. "Very true. But for now we're going to have lunch and lay all our cards on the table."

Sunny, her shoulder under her grandfather, nearly staggered at the news. *Lord, have mercy… Honesty at last?*

"Good! I've been waiting to do just that," Grant said with relief.

Sunny shot Grant a fulminating glance while speaking to Nathan. "I think you should rest for a while after lunch."

"Not till after we settle things." Her grandfather's dictate was firm.

"Well, I—"

"I'm hungry enough to eat bear," her granddad interrupted. "Let's talk later."

Sunny gritted her teeth. Never had she wanted to scream like a banshee, but she stuffed it all down. She might as well be talking to one of those stone cliffs.

Lord, I need Your help…boy oh boy, do I need Your help! Please, I can't handle this situation, nor do I want to listen to a single explanation of that—that good-looking, oh-so-charming liar!

She turned her back while Grant helped her granddad into her apartment, just to let Grant know she was

still annoyed with him. Then while the two men settled
on the old sofa, she started preparing lunch.

As she opened a couple of cans of tuna, her mind
whirled, her thoughts tumbling like leaves on a
stormy day.

*That's what you've always longed for, haven't you?
A family. You wanted all the emotions...the love, the
fondness...even the annoyances and irritations. You
wanted someone of your own, to know just one member
of your family...to know your inheritance of family...*

But I didn't want...

Betrayal...

Betrayal was the word that came to mind. The thought
hurt so much it dug a hole in her heart. It deepened when
she realized just how far her emotions for Grant had
gone. She was very much in love with him. Now she felt
cut off, as she'd done when a kid. Was she a nothing?
Good for fill-in but not good enough to count first.

She wanted to cry...to howl at the moon.

She wanted with all her being to be number one in
someone's eyes. She wanted someone...someone who
loved her, to whom she was more important than life.

Then Nathan's gruff voice cut through the confused
thoughts. "Do you love her?"

What? Who was Granddad talking about? She
glanced over her shoulder.

"More than life." Grant's voice deepened with emotion.

Sunny stopped chopping celery to listen.

"Just want to know your intentions." Grandfather's
voice grew gruffer.

Intentions! *Intentions?* She was twenty-six years

old…was her granddad talking about her? Did he have the right to ask such a question? Why were they talking to each other and leaving her out?

A white-hot explosion filled her like a volcanic eruption. She slapped the knife down on the counter and whirled, shooting sparks from her gaze, her hands on her hips to look the two men over.

"All right, you two, that's it! I want to understand all this right now. Why? Why the charade? Why all this…this crazy pretense?"

Nathan spoke. "Had to know if you were a schemer, Sunny. After my money. Didn't know you at all…wanted to know what kind of woman you were."

"Couldn't you have just *asked* me?"

Nathan shook his head. "Not after that Frankie fella tried to get money out of me."

She put a hand to her head. "Who's Frankie? I don't understand."

"We didn't know about you, Shirley and me. We'd of been proud of having you as a grandchild. Johnny died so suddenly like that…it was a shock an' all."

"I guess that was Mom's fault that you didn't know. She thought— Never mind." She shook her head. "What about this Frankie guy?"

"Okay. Well, Frankie Brewster. He was a friend of Johnny's. Didn't like him much. Still don't, as a matter of fact, but anyway, he came around about last February, chatty and all. He told me about you."

"Well, then—"

"Showed me pictures of Johnny with your mom. But then, it was a shake-down. Frankie wanted money to put me in touch with you. To tell me where I could find you."

"You're not making this up?" She pulled a kitchen chair free and sank down. She could only measure the truth with her heart. "It's true?"

Grant muttered, "Yes, it's true, Sunny. I was here when Frankie came out, and your granddad wouldn't talk without me present. I didn't like Frankie, either."

She gazed at him, confusion dwelling in her eyes.

Grant stared back, his blue gaze blazing with apology...and sorrow...and love.

And begging for understanding. Her heart turned over and some of her anger melted.

"I want to explain my part in all this. Will you listen now?"

She slowly nodded. He scooted forward on his seat. She thought she could at least listen. That didn't take much...only half her heart.

Grant continued. "I know there's no real excuse for the lies I've told...or rather, the truth I've avoided. Or the secrets I've kept. But your granddad wanted—"

"Now wait a minute," Sunny bit out, her temper flaring once more. "Wait just a dog-gone minute. Don't blame this all on my grandfather."

"Sunny, let him explain!" said Nathan.

She shushed him with a sharp wave of her hand, holding Grant's gaze.

"You never told me my grandfather was dead. You never said he wasn't, or anything like that. You just said he had made a deal to sell this place to you. The land and all."

"Well, that's true, but I—"

"You simply avoided telling me that he was alive!" she accused.

"Yes, I did that, but your grandfather wanted—"

"You *lied!*"

Grant merely dropped his lashes. His shame and embarrassment were evident.

What was left of her anger was melting.

"Now, Sunny, no, he didn't," Nathan put in quickly. "He just didn't tell you all the truth. I had to find out what kind of woman I was dealing with, didn't I? That Frankie guy wanted my money, I thought maybe you did, too."

"What money are you talking about?" Confused once more, she rose and walked about the room. "Is there more than this resort?"

"Um…yeah, I got a few parcels of land about the lake." Nathan's head bobbed in positive inclination. "Oh, this is yours, all right. You can do with it whatever you want to—I wouldn't take it away from you—but I'm going to Arizona for the winters."

"Ah, I see. Now what about this Frankie guy?"

"Well, after he came to see me, I got to thinking about Johnny's wild days. He talked once about your mom, and he coulda fathered a child, I thought. But I wasn't going to pay that Frankie to tell me about it. So I hired a detective. He came up with you…"

Sunny stared out at the lake. "I suppose I believe you. I guess I was so thrilled with owning something my grandparents' valued, it made my logic fuzzy. I was starting to dream of—"

"Glad the truth is out," said Nathan. "I was getting fuzzy with all the playacting myself."

Grant spoke. "Dream of what, Sunny?"

"On, nothing. I—it was me… I was just hoping, that's all. Just dreaming that after the gathering of that youth group…well, I thought we might make a team for foster kids…"

"What are you talking about? What foster kids?"

"Oh, any of them. My foster family, for instance. I thought we could bring them down for a vacation or something. There are lots of foster kids everywhere. I thought maybe we could bring some of those kids here, give them a good time. They'd love it. You could show them how to fish and how to ride. They'd just think they were in paradise, that's what they'd think. I—I—"

"What are you talking about, Sunny? I never said anything about making this place for foster kids."

"No, no. You didn't say that at all. That was just dumb me…so foolish to think…it was only my dream."

"But it's a fine idea." Was he saying that to appease her? She didn't know, but she watched him as he came closer.

"Now I'll take this opportunity to ask it again, Grant." Nathan frowned. "What are your intentions toward Sunny?"

"What?" Sunny squealed, her head turned toward Nathan.

"To love her as she should be loved, that's my intention."

"Well, praise God, that's something," said Nathan.

Grant's head whipped around, too, surprise on his face. "You! Praising God?"

"Well, my granddaughter does."

"But you never gave Him any consideration before—"

"Yeah, but I never experienced a miracle before, either. Been thinking about it all night. Finding Sunny was like God coming down, using an odd situation like that Frankie fella to tell me about her, then finding that, sure enough, I got a granddaughter. Someone of my own lineage. Now, what were you saying?"

Sunny blinked. Grant made a face and pulled on his ear.

"I was saying I'll love Sunny for all my life—"

"What?" exclaimed Sunny, her attention back to Grant. Her mouth fell open slightly. Had she fallen into a rabbit hole? Grant lightly kissed her, sliding his arms about her.

"With a lifetime of devotion" he leaned into her ear, whispering, "and heart-stopping emotion."

"Oh…" She leaned back, his arms holding her, and watched his sky-blue eyes, looking for honesty. What she saw resonated with a heart-pounding truth.

"I love you, Sunny," Grant said, tightening his arms.

He did love her, Sunny's stunned mind accepted. He did. Her heart beating lightly, her hopes rose high.

"More than I thought I could love anyone."

"You really do?"

"You're my life! I'll never, ever lie to you again. That's a solemn promise. I'll always be honest in every aspect of our lives, if you marry me. On the Lord's name, I promise. Please marry me?"

"Yes," Sunny whispered.

"Yes?" Grant began to grin.

"Yes!" shouted Nathan. He bounced as best he could, his cast keeping him down. "At last… And I can trust you to keep Sunshine Acres intact with Grant's Retreat? Don't care how many foster kids you take in, as long as you give me some great-grandkids to spoil."

Neither heard him as their focus centered on each other. Sunny rose to her toes to give Grant her mouth.

"Oh, I do love you so," Sunny said.

"Thank God you do," said Nathan. "Thank God you do!"

Sunny's chuckles began low, then roared into laughter.

She at last had a family, with all the emotions that possession entailed. She entertained the best in happiness.

"Yes…thank God."

* * * * *

Dear Reader,

It's always fun to write about a place that was familiar in your childhood. Many vacations were spent "down at the lake" with family and friends when our children were little. A few days at the Lake of the Ozarks can still bring a welcome break, and we are planning a trip down now with our extended family.

Long discussions and much sharing goes on in between boat, jet ski and parasailing outings, and during hikes and meals. In the midst of all that fun and togetherness, we often talk about our faith and how God carries us through when things aren't so sunny. We see the beauty that He created in the surrounding hills and valleys, sunsets and moon rises, and remind ourselves that He is in control. We ask a blessing at the beginning of each meal to acknowledge Him. It's important to us to keep Him in our lives during vacation just as we do every day. And we praise God!

I hope you enjoy Sunny and Grant as much as I did. You may write me at Ruth Scofield, P.O. Box 1221, Blue Springs, MO 64013. Please enclose a SASE.

Ruth Scofield

Love Inspired®

FIRST MATES

BY

CECELIA
DOWDY

Cruising the Caribbean was just what Rainy Jackson needed
to get over her faithless ex-fiancé…and meeting handsome
fellow passenger Winston Michaels didn't hurt, either! As a
new Christian, Winston was looking to reflect on his own
losses. Yet as the two spent some time together both on the
ship and back home in Miami, he soon realized he wanted
Rainy along to share his life voyage.

Don't miss FIRST MATES

On sale February 2005

Available at your favorite retail outlet.

Take 2 inspirational love stories FREE!

PLUS get a FREE surprise gift!

Mail to Steeple Hill Reader Service™

In U.S.
3010 Walden Ave.
P.O. Box 1867
Buffalo, NY 14240-1867

In Canada
P.O. Box 609
Fort Erie, Ontario
L2A 5X3

YES! Please send me 2 free Love Inspired® novels and my free surprise gift. After receiving them, if I don't wish to receive anymore, I can return the shipping statement marked cancel. If I don't cancel, I will receive 4 brand-new novels every month, before they're available in stores! Bill me at the low price of $4.24 each in the U.S. and $4.74 each in Canada, plus 25¢ shipping and handling and applicable sales tax, if any*. That's the complete price and a savings of over 10% off the cover prices—quite a bargain! I understand that accepting the books and gift places me under no obligation ever to buy any books. I can always return a shipment and cancel at any time. Even if I never buy another book from Steeple Hill, the 2 free books and the surprise gift are mine to keep forever.

113 IDN DZ9M
313 IDN DZ9N

Name	(PLEASE PRINT)	
Address	Apt. No.	
City	State/Prov.	Zip/Postal Code

Not valid to current Love Inspired® subscribers.

Want to try two free books from another series?
Call 1-800-873-8635 or visit www.morefreebooks.com.

* Terms and prices are subject to change without notice. Sales tax applicable in New York. Canadian residents will be charged applicable provincial taxes and GST. All orders subject to approval. Offer limited to one per household.

® are registered trademarks owned and used by the trademark owner and or its licensee.

INTLI04R   ©2004 Steeple Hill

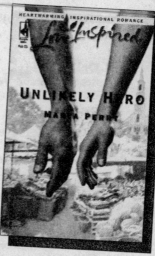